RETURN TO THRUSH GREEN

Miss Read

Illustrated by J. S. Goodall

HOUGHTON MIFFLIN COMPANY

Boston   New York

First Houghton Mifflin paperback edition 2002
First American edition 1979
Copyright © 1978 by Miss Read
All rights reserved

For information about permission to reproduce
selections from this book, write to Permissions,
Houghton Mifflin Company, 215 Park Avenue South,
New York, New York 10003.

Visit our Web site: www.houghtonmifflinbooks.com.

Library of Congress Cataloging-in-Publication Data is available.
ISBN 0-618-21914-5

Printed in the United States of America
QUM 10 9 8 7 6 5 4 3

International Praise for Miss Read

"Miss Read reminds us of what is really important. And if we can't live in her world, it's certainly a comforting place to visit." — *USA Today*

"An affectionate, humorous, and gently charming chronicle . . . sometimes funny, sometimes touching, always appealing."
— *New York Times*

"[Miss Read] has achieved a sort of universality."
— *Chicago Sunday Tribune*

"Miss Read has three great gifts — an unerring intuition about human frailty, a healthy irony, and, surprisingly, an almost beery sense of humor. As a result, her villages, the rush of the sun and snow through venerable elms, and the children themselves all miraculously manage to blend into a charming and lasting whole." — *The New Yorker*

"Humor guides her pen but charity steadies it . . . delightful."
— *Times Literary Supplement*

"We need more books like this . . . quiet, homey stories about down-to-earth people." — *Anniston Star*

"Miss Read has created an orderly universe in which people are kind and conscientious and cherish virtues and manners now considered antiquated elsewhere . . . An occasional visit . . . offers a restful change from the frenetic pace of the contemporary world."
— *Publishers Weekly*

"What you will find in the novels of Miss Read is an aura of warm happiness." — *Columbus Dispatch*

"Miss Read has created a world of innocent integrity in almost perfect prose consisting of wit, humor, and wisdom in equal measure."
— *Cleveland Plain Dealer*

"Someone has said she writes for ordinary people extraordinarily; when I read her I keep thinking of the acute perception and wit of Jane Austen. [Miss Read] is unique, and oh, so pleasant to read."
— *Chattanooga Times*

"Miss Read [possesses] a tranquil eye in the midst of our loud and windy times." — *Patriot Ledger*

Books by Miss Read

To
Sir Robert Lusty,
whose early encouragement
began it all

To
Sir Robert Lusty,
whose early encouragement
began it all

CONTENTS

Part One

Travelling Hopefully

Part Two

Change at Thrush Green

Part Three

Safe Arrival

Epilogue

Part One
Travelling Hopefully

1 Spring Afternoon

THE finest house at Thrush Green, everyone agreed, was that occupied by Joan and Edward Young. Built of honey-coloured Cotswold stone, some hundred or so years ago, it had a beautiful matching tiled roof, mottled with a patina of lichen and moss. It looked southward, across the length of the green, to the little market town of Lulling hidden in the valley half a mile away.

The house had been built by a mill owner who had made a comfortable fortune at the woollen mill which straddled the river Pleshey a mile or two west of Lulling. It was large enough to house his family of six, and three resident maids. A range of stone-built stables, a coach house and tack room, stood a little way from the house, and at right angles to it. Above the stable was the bothy, where the groom-cum-coachman slept, and immediately above the bedroom was the stable clock.

The Youngs often wondered how on earth people managed without such storage space. Nowadays, the buildings were filled with furniture awaiting repair, lawn-mowers, deck-chairs, tea-chests full of bottling equipment or archaic kitchen utensils which 'might come in useful one day', two deep freezers, a decrepit work bench and an assortment of outgrown toys, such as a tricycle and a rocking horse, the property of

Paul Young, their only child. Everything needing a temporary
home found its way into the stable and then became a per-
manency. Sagging wicker garden chairs, shabby trunks, cat
baskets, camping stoves, old tennis racquets, fishing waders,
and Paul's pram, unused for nine years, were housed here,
jostling each other, and coated with dust, bird droppings and
the débris from ancient nests in the beams above.

'If ever we had to move, said Edward to Joan one sunny
afternoon, 'I can't think how we'd begin to sort out this lot.'

He was looking for space in which to dump two sacks of
garden fertilizer.

'Those new flats in Lulling,' he went on, 'have exactly
three cupboards in each. People seem to cope all right. How
do we get so much clobber?'

'It's a law of nature,' Joan replied. 'Abhorring a vacuum and
all that. However much space you have, you fill it.'

She pushed an unsteady pile of old copies of *Country Life*
nearer to a mildewed camp bed.

'I suppose we could set a match to it,' suggested Edward,
dragging the first sack to a resting place beside some croquet
mallets. There was a rustling sound and a squeak.

'That was a mouse!' said Joan, retreating hastily.

'Rats, more like,' commented Edward, heaving along the
second sack. 'Come on, my dear. Let's leave them to it. I'm
supposed to be meeting Bodger at two-thirty and it's two
o'clock already.'

Together they made their way back towards the house.

When her husband had gone, Joan sat on the garden seat to
enjoy the spring sunshine. Cold winds had delayed the opening

of many flowers. Certainly no daffodils had 'come before the swallow dared to take the winds of March with beauty'.

Here we are, thought Joan, surveying the garden through half-closed eyes, in mid-April, and the daffodils and narcissi are only just in their prime. Would the primroses be starring the banks along the lane to Nidden, she wondered? As children, she and her sister Ruth had reckoned the first outing to pick primroses as the true herald of spring.

How lucky they had been to have grandparents living at Thrush Green, thought Joan, looking back to those happy days with affection. She and Ruth lived most of the year in Ealing, where their father owned a furniture shop. They lived comfortably in a house built in King Edward's reign. The garden was large for a town house. The common was nearby, and Kew Gardens a bus ride away. But to the little girls, such amenities were definitely second-best.

'It's not *the country*!' they protested. 'Why can't we live in *the country*? Why don't we go to Thrush Green for good?'

'Because my living's here,' said Mr Bassett, smiling. 'There are four of us to keep, and the house and garden to care for, and your schooling to be paid. If I don't work, then we have nothing. You must think yourselves lucky to be able to go to Thrush Green as often as you do.'

He too adored Thrush Green, and when his parents died, it became his. Barely fifty, he intended to continue to live and work in Ealing. By this time, Joan had married Edward Young, an architect in Lulling known to the Bassetts since childhood, and the young couple had lived in the house ever since.

'But the day I retire,' Mr Bassett had said, 'I'll be down to take over, you know!'

'I'll build a house in readiness,' promised Edward. That was over ten years ago, thought Joan, stretching out her legs into the sunshine, and we still have not built it. Perhaps we should think about it, instead of drifting on from day to day. Father must be in his sixties now, and had not been well this winter. The time must come when he decided to retire, and only right that he should come to Thrush Green to enjoy his heritage. They had been wonderfully blessed to have had so long in this lovely place.

The telephone bell broke in upon her musing, and she left the sunshine to answer it.

Some two hundred yards away, the children of Thrush Green Village School were enjoying the first really warm and sunny playtime of the year.

Squealing and skipping, jostling and jumping, they celebrated the return of spring with youthful exuberance. Little Miss Fogerty, teacup in hand, watched their activities with fond indulgence. She had coped with playground duty now for over thirty years. The mothers and fathers of some of these screaming infants had once cavorted here under her kindly eye. She lifted her wrinkled face to the sun, and watched the rooks flying to the tall trees on the road to Nidden. Two of them carried twigs in their beaks. It was good to see them refurbishing their nests, she thought, and better still to note that they were building high this year. A sure sign, old country-men said, of a fine summer to come. Well, it could not be too hot for her old bones, thought Miss Fogerty. She must think about looking out her cotton dresses. What a blessing she had decided not to shorten them last year! Hems were definitely

mid-calf this season, and very becoming too after those
dreadful mini-skirts which were downright improper, and must
have given many a fast young man ideas of the worst sort.

A windswept child pranced up to her.

'Finished, miss? Give us yer cup then!'

Miss Fogerty held her cup and saucer well above the child's
head, and looked sternly at his flushed face.

'"May I take your cup, *Miss Fogerty*," is the way to ask,
Frederick,' she said reprovingly. 'Just repeat it, please.'

'May I take your cup, Miss Fogerty?' repeated Frederick
meekly. 'And I never meant no harm, miss.'

Miss Fogerty smiled and put the empty cup and saucer into
his hands.

'I'm quite sure of that, Frederick dear, but there is a right
and wrong way of doing everything, and you chose the wrong
way first.'

'Yes, miss,' agreed Frederick, holding the china against his
jersey, and setting off across the playground to the lobby where
the washing up was done.

Miss Fogerty glanced at her wrist watch. Only three
minutes more and she must blow her whistle.

There would be nice time for *The Tailor of Gloucester* before
the end of the afternoon. She thought, with pleasure, of the
scores of children she had introduced to Beatrix Potter. How
many times, she wondered, had she carried the little picture
showing the embroidered waistcoat round the room, watching
each child's face rapt with wonder at the smallness of the
stitches and beauty of the design.

And her new classroom was so pleasant! For years she had
worked in the infants' room to the right of the lobby in the

original village school building. Now the new classroom at the
rear of the school was hers alone, complete with its own wash-
basins and lavatories, so that there was no need for any of the
babies to brave the weather when crossing the playground, as
in the old days.

The new room was a constant delight to her. The big
windows faced southwest across the valley towards Lulling
Woods. Bean and pea seeds, as well as mustard and cress
growing on flannel in saucers, flourished on the sunny windowsill, and it was delightful to stand, back against the glass, and
feel the hot sun warming one's shoulder blades through one's
cardigan.

It had been good of Miss Watson, her headmistress, to let
her have the room. She could so easily have appropriated it
for her own class had she wished. But there, thought loyal
little Miss Fogerty, Miss Watson would never do a thing like
that! There could not be a better headmistress in the whole of
the United Kingdom! It was a privilege to be on her staff.

Miss Fogerty fished up the whistle from the recesses of
her twin-set and blew a loud blast. Three-quarters of the
playground pandemonium ceased. Miss Fogerty's grey eyes,
turning like twin lighthouse beams, round her territory,
quenched the last few decibels of noise.

'You may lead in, children,' she called. 'My class last this
time.'

And as the school filed indoors, she followed the youngest
children across the playground to the beautiful new terrapin
building where *The Tailor of Gloucester* was waiting on her
desk.

*   *   *

From her bedroom window across the green, Winnie Bailey watched Miss Fogerty at her duties. Since her husband's death, she had found herself observing other people with an interest which she had not had time to indulge during the years of the doctor's last illness.

She missed him more than she could say. The fact that their last few months together had involved her in nursing Donald day and night, made their home seem even more lonely now that he had gone.

The tributes she had received at his death, and still received daily from those who had known him, gave Winnie Bailey much needed comfort. He had been a dear man all his life, and a very handsome one when young, but it was his complete dedication to the task of healing which had endeared him to the people of Lulling and Thrush Green. Every day, Sundays included, Donald Bailey had visited Lulling Cottage Hospital, until infirmity had overtaken him. His young partner Doctor Lovell, married to Ruth, Joan Young's sister, knew how lucky he was to have watched and learnt from such a splendid man as his senior partner.

'Never appear to be in a hurry,' the old man had said to him. 'Listen to their tales, no matter how irrelevant they may seem at the time. You'll learn more that way about your patient than any number of tests at the clinic. Mind and matter are interwoven to an extent that none of us truly appreciates. If you are going to expect exactly the same reaction to the same treatment in every case, then you might just as well become a mechanic.'

Doctor Lovell's car backed cautiously away from the surgery into the road. He looked up and saw Winnie at the window, and waved cheerfully. He had probably called for medicines, thought Winnie, and was off to pay a few afternoon calls before evening surgery.

A bent figure was hurrying across Thrush Green from the church. It was Albert Piggott, sexton and so-called caretaker of St Andrew's, and he was obviously intent upon waylaying the unsuspecting doctor.

His cracked voice floated up to Winnie at the window.

'Doctor! Doctor! You got somethin' for me choobs? They've gone again!'

Doctor Lovell wound down the car window and said something which Winnie could not hear. She moved away hastily, not wishing to appear inquisitive, and made her way downstairs, where Jenny, her maid and friend for many years, was getting the tea-tray ready.

I am a lucky woman, thought Winnie, to be able to continue to live at Thrush Green among old friends, to have Jenny with me for company, and to see Donald's work carried on so conscientiously by John Lovell and his new young assistant. How pleased Donald would have been!

Albert Piggott, returning from his foray upon the doctor's car, looked upon the closed door of the Two Pheasants and thought sadly how far distant opening time was. They did things better abroad, he believed. Opened all day, so he'd heard. Now we were all in this Common Market perhaps we'd follow the foreigners' good example.

At that moment, the landlord of the Two Pheasants struggled through the wicket gate at the side of the public house, bearing two hanging baskets.

'Well, Albert,' said Mr Jones, depositing the baskets at his feet, 'how's tricks?'

'Chest's bad,' said Albert flatly.

'Always is, ain't it? Time you was used to it.'

'That's right,' growled Albert. 'Show plenty of sympathy!' He surveyed the two baskets.

'You being fool enough to put them geraniums out already?' he continued. 'I s'pose you know we're due for plenty more frost.'

'They won't hurt under the eaves,' said the landlord. 'Got some shelter, see?'

'Might well get one tonight,' went on Albert, with every

appearance of satisfaction. 'My choobs have been playin' up somethin' cruel. Went to see the doctor about 'em.'

'Ah! I saw you,' said Mr Jones. 'Holding up the poor chap when he was just off to see them as is really ill.'

Albert did not reply, but commented by spitting a flashing arc towards the churchyard wall.

The landlord pulled out the wooden bench and began to mount upon it.

'Wouldn't want to give me a hand-up with the baskets, I suppose?'

Albert looked at him sourly.

'You supposes right,' he said. 'I've got work of me own to do, thank you.'

He shuffled off towards his cottage which stood next door.

'Miserable old faggot,' said Mr Jones dismounting, and making towards the baskets. He made the comment quietly, but just loud enough to carry to Albert's ears as he opened his front door.

After the fresh air of Thrush Green, even Albert noticed that his kitchen seemed stuffy.

The general opinion of his neighbours was that Albert's home was absolutely filthy and smelt accordingly. No one had ever seen a window open, and the door was only opened long enough to allow the entry or exit of its master's unwashed body.

Albert sat down heavily in the greasy armchair, and began to unlace his boots. He removed them with a sigh of relief, and lay back, his gaze resting upon a pile of dirty crockery which littered the draining-board. He supposed he would have to tackle that sometime, he thought morosely. And get himself a bite to eat.

He became conscious of his hunger, and thought of Nelly, his wife, who had left him over a year ago to share life with the oil man somewhere further south.

'Nothin' but a common trollop!' muttered Albert aloud. 'But, golly, she could cook!'

He thought of the succulent steak and kidney pies which had emerged steaming from the now cold and dusty kitchen range. She made a fine stew too, remembered Albert, his gastric juices working strongly, and liver and bacon pudding with haricot beans. As for her treacle tarts, and rice puddings with a nice brown crinkly skin of butter and nutmeg on top, they were real works of art.

She had a way with mashed potatoes too, beating an egg into them so that the saucepan was full of light fluff, slightly creamy in colour and texture. He could do with a plateful of Nelly's cooking at the moment, he thought wistfully.

He rose from the chair and went to the cupboard where he found a piece of bread. He spread it with a dollop of dripping from a stone jamjar, and began to munch disconsolately. It wasn't right that a man had to find his own vittles, especially one who was delicate. One with ailing tubes, like himself, for instance.

Still, cooking wasn't everything, Albert told himself, wiping his hands down his trousers. She might be a good cook, his Nelly, he would be the first to give you that, but what a Tartar too! What a temper! And sly with it! Look at the way she'd been carrying on with that blighted oil man behind his back! He wished him joy of her, the wicked hussy. He hoped he'd had a lashing from her tongue by now, so that he'd see what he'd taken on, and what her lawful wedded husband had had to put up with.

He filled the kettle and put it on to boil. By the time he'd washed up, and had a snooze, it would be near enough time to go and lock up the church and see that all was straight for the night.

And after that, thought Albert, the Two Pheasants would be open!

Life suddenly became warmer and sunnier as Albert advanced bravely upon the sticky horrors piled in the sink.

2 Doctor's Prescription

WHILE the children of Miss Fogerty's class listened to the story of *The Tailor of Gloucester*, and Albert Piggott awaited opening time, Joan Young was busy preparing a salad.

As she washed lettuce and cut tomatoes her thoughts turned time and time again to her parents and her old home in Ealing. She was vaguely puzzled by this. She had an uncomfortable feeling that perhaps something was wrong, and tried to persuade herself that the fact that she had been thinking of her father's heritage, after Edward's return to work that afternoon, simply accounted for this present preoccupation.

But somehow she was not convinced. She was the last person to be telepathic, or to believe in such nebulous things as thought-transference. Nevertheless, the malaise continued, and for two pins she would have left her salad-making and rung her parents there and then.

'What nonsense!' she told herself. 'They would think I'd gone mad. I should have heard soon enough if anything were wrong!'

She began to slice cucumber with swift efficient strokes.

Some sixty miles away, Joan's father, Robert Bassett, listened to some very unwelcome truths spoken by his doctor.

'These X-rays show that that chest of yours needs a lot of care. And I'm not happy about your heart. I'm not suggesting that you should consider yourself an invalid, but frankly it's time you gave up work.'

'But it's quite impossible –' began his patient, and was interrupted by a violent spell of coughing.

The doctor watched gravely until the attack had passed. He said nothing, but continued to look steadily at the older man.

'Dammit all,' wheezed Robert, 'it's only this confounded cough that makes me so tired! I'm fine otherwise. Look here, I've a business to run, you know.'

'Someone else will have to run it anyway in a few months,' said the doctor soberly.

He rose from the bedside and went to look out of the window at the neat suburban garden. Robert Bassett, shocked by the last few words, addressed the doctor's straight back.

'You don't mean that?'

The doctor swung round.

'I do indeed. All the tests we have done, these X-rays, and my knowledge of you over the last six years show that you are running yourself into the ground at an alarming rate. You need rest, cleaner air and more quiet than Ealing can give you, and a complete removal from sight and sound of your work. If you refuse to take my advice, I don't give you twelve months. It may sound brutal, my old friend, but that's the position.'

There was a short silence. Somewhere in the distance, a train hooted, and nearer at hand a lorry changed gear and ground away up the hill outside.

'I just can't take it in,' whispered the sick man.

'You own a house somewhere in the west, don't you? Can you go and stay there for a time?'

'Now do you mean?'

'Not immediately. You're going to have a week or two in that bed, with a daily visit from me. It will give you time to get used to the idea of moving, and to put things straight this end.'

'But what about my business?'

'Surely, there's someone there who can take over?'

'I suppose so,' said Robert slowly. 'It's just that I've never really considered the matter.'

The doctor patted his patient's hand, and rose to go.

'Well, consider it now, and cheer up. You'd like to go to this country house of yours, I take it?'

'Of course I would,' said Robert. 'I've always promised myself a retirement at Thrush Green.'

'Good, good! That's grand news.'

He picked up his case, and smiled at his patient.

'What's more,' said Robert, 'I've a son-in-law who is the doctor there.'

'Better still! I'll be in touch with him, no doubt, when the time comes. Meanwhile, you stay here and get some sleep. I'll be in tomorrow.'

He closed the door behind him, leaving his patient in mental turmoil.

'Sleep!' muttered Robert crossly. 'What a hope! I must get Milly to ring the office straightaway and get young Frank to come over.'

He sat up suddenly, and was reminded of his weakness by a severe pain in the chest.

Rubbing it ruefully, he thought of further arrangements to be made.

'We'd better warn Joan and Edward, poor dears, that they may have a convalescent father on their hands in the near future.'

Nevertheless, the thought of Thrush Green in spring sunshine, gave comfort to the invalid in the midst of his trials.

In Miss Fogerty's classroom *The Tailor of Gloucester* had been returned to the shelf, the children had stacked their diminutive chairs upon the tables, leaving the floor clear for the cleaner's ministrations later, and now stood, hands together and eyes closed, waiting for their teacher to give the note for grace.

Now the day is over,
Night is drawing nigh,
Shadows of the evening
Steal across the sky.
Now the darkness gathers
Stars begin to peep,
Birds and beasts and flowers
Soon will be asleep.
      Amen

They sang much too loudly for Miss Fogerty's peace of mind. It sounded irreverent, she felt, but she had not the heart to reprove them, knowing how eagerly they were looking forward to running home through the first of the really warm days of spring.

She thought, not for the first time, that this particular closing hymn was not one of her favourites. That line 'Stars begin to peep', for instance, was a little premature at three-thirty, except in December perhaps, and in any case the word 'peep' seemed a trifle coy. But there, Miss Watson wanted the children to use that hymn, and she must fall in with her wishes in these little matters.

'Hands away! Good afternoon, children!' said Miss Fogerty briskly. 'Straight home now, and no shouting near the school windows. The big girls and boys are still working, remember.'

They streamed from the room comparatively quietly, and

across the playground towards Thrush Green. Daisies starred
the greensward, and the sticky buds of the chestnut trees were
beginning to break into miniature fans of grey-green. The
children raced happily to meet all the glory of a spring
afternoon.

All except Timmy Thomas, always a rebel, who saw fit to
stand beneath Miss Watson's window, put two fingers into
his mouth and produce an ear-splitting whistle.

He was gratified to see his headmistress's face appear at the
window. She shook her head at him sternly and pointed
towards the gate. Miss Fogerty had emerged from her classroom, and also exhorted him to depart immediately.

Grinning, he went.

'That boy,' said Miss Watson later, 'will become a very
unpleasant leader of students, or some such, as far as I can see!'

'He might make a happy marriage,' observed Miss Fogerty,
more charitably, 'and settle down.'

'It seems a long time to wait,' commented her headmistress
tartly.

One of the first of Miss Fogerty's pupils to reach home, was
young Jeremy Prior who lived just across Thrush Green at
Tullivers, a house as venerable as the Youngs', although not
quite so imposing.

Jeremy enjoyed life at Thrush Green. His mother Phil had
married for the second time, and his stepfather, Frank Hurst,
was a man whose company he enjoyed. His own father had
been killed in a car crash, but before that had happened he
had left home to live in France with another woman, so that
the child's memories of him were dim. Frank had given him

the affection and care which he needed in his early years, and Jeremy flourished in the happy atmosphere surrounding him at Thrush Green.

Now, as he opened the gate, he was conscious of his mother talking to friends in the garden.

One was Winnie Bailey, their next-door neighbour. The other was Ruth Lovell, the doctor's wife, and clutching her hand was Mary, her two-year-old daughter.

As soon as the toddler saw Jeremy she broke away from her mother and charged over the flower beds to greet the boy, babbling incoherently, fat arms outstretched.

'*Mary*!' shouted Ruth. '*Not* over the garden!'

But she was ignored. Her daughter by now had Jeremy's legs in a rapturous embrace which nearly brought him to the ground.

'Is it as late as that?' exclaimed Winnie. 'I must get back. Jenny has gone down to Lulling, and I'm supposed to be keeping an eye on a fruit cake in the oven.'

She hurried away and they heard the click of the next-door gate as she returned to her duties.

'How are things working out there?' asked Ruth.

'Very well, I gather,' said Phil. 'It was a marvellous idea to invite Jenny to live with her. At one stage I was afraid that Winnie might think of moving into a smaller house, perhaps near her sister. We should have missed her horribly, and I think she would have been lost without Thrush Green.'

'I'm sure of it. We're lucky to live here. Joan and I always thought it was the best place on earth when we were children. I can't say that my opinion has changed much.'

She walked towards her daughter who was rolling over

and over on the grass, being helped by Jeremy.

'Come along, Mary. We're off to see Aunt Joan.'

'No! Stay here,' said Mary, stopping abruptly, her frock under her armpits and an expanse of fat stomach exposed to view. Her expression was mutinous.

'No nonsense now! We've got to collect the magazines.'

'Why not let her stop here while you see Joan?' suggested Phil, in a low tone. 'Jeremy would love to play with her for a while.'

'That's so kind. I won't be more than a few minutes.'

She turned towards the gate.

'Do you mind, Jeremy?' she called.

'I'll show her my new fort,' said Jeremy enthusiastically. 'It's got Crusaders and Saracens, and lots of flags and horses and swords.'

'Mind she doesn't swallow them,' advised Ruth. 'You don't want to lose any.'

She waved to the potential sword-swallower and made her way across the green to her sister's.

Joan Young was sitting in the hall when Ruth arrived. She was listening intently to the telephone, her face grave.

Ruth was about to tiptoe away, but Joan covered the mouthpiece with her hand, and motioned her sister to take a seat.

'It's mother. Tell you in a minute.'

Ruth perched on the oak settle, and fell to admiring the black and white tiles of the floor, and the elegant staircase, which always gave her pleasure.

'Do you want a word with Ruth? She's just dropped in.'

Silence reigned while Joan listened again.

'No, no. All right, darling. I'll tell her, and you know we'll look forward to seeing you both. Yes, *any time*! Give him our love.'

She replaced the receiver and looked at Ruth.

'Poor Dad, he's pretty weak evidently. Bed for a week or two, and then his doctor wants him to come here for a rest.'

She stood up abruptly.

'Come in the garden, Ruth. I've left a cookery book on the seat, and I probably shan't remember it until it pours with rain in the middle of the night.'

'How bad is he?' asked Ruth, following her.

'Mother was calm about it, but sounded anxious. It seems he's had this bronchial trouble most of the winter, but wouldn't give up. I'll be glad to get him here. Mother must need a rest too. Dash it all, they're both around seventy.'

They sat down on the garden seat, and Joan nursed the cookery book.

'Shall we go up tomorrow to see him?' said Ruth.

'Mother says not to. He's not in any danger, but the doctor wants him to be kept quiet.'

She began to laugh.

'Poor Mum, trying to stop him working! As it is, she's had to ring Frank to give all sorts of messages about the office.'

'It's time he retired,' agreed her sister. 'Perhaps this will make him think about it.'

'Funnily enough,' said Joan, 'they've been in my mind a lot today. Probably because Edward said something about moving. It's about time we built a house of our own. We may have to now. Heaven knows we've been lucky to stay here so long.'

'Dad won't let you move,' said Ruth shrewdly. At times she saw more clearly than her older sister, who usually led the way.

'But he'll have to!' replied Joan, beginning to look slightly agitated. 'If he's to have a quiet life from now on, then it's only right that he should come back to his own home.'

'Maybe,' agreed Ruth. 'He'll be willing to come to Thrush Green, I have no doubt, but he won't let you give up your home, you'll see.'

'But where else is there for him? We've always known that they would retire here.'

'Don't forget that Dad hasn't yet said he will retire. So far, he's simply having a short convalescence here. I shouldn't take too many leaps ahead, Joan. Things will work out, you'll see.'

She rose to her feet.

'I came for the magazines really, and then I must collect Mary before she drives Jeremy Prior mad. Noble boy, he's showing her his fort. I tremble to think how much of it is broken already.'

They made their way back to the house, and collected the pile of magazines from the hall table. A dozen or so inhabitants of Thrush Green had begun this communal magazine effort during the war, each contributing one journal and passing the collection from one to the other, and the custom had continued.

'I'll walk across the green with you,' said Joan. 'It's marvellous to feel the sun really warm again after months of shivering.'

They paused at the roadside and Joan gazed across the grass towards the church.

'Do you realise that we shall have the Curdles' fair here again on May the first? Only another week or so. Won't it be lovely to see Ben and Molly Curdle again? I still miss her.'

'The only comfort is that she's a lot happier with her Ben than she was with that ghastly father of hers, Albert Piggott. Isn't that him over there in the churchyard?'

'Looks like it. Waiting for the Two Pheasants to open no doubt.'

'Mary is going to the fair this year,' said Ruth. 'Perhaps we could make up a party with Jeremy and Paul?'

'Yes, let's. Though I may have the parents here by then, of course.'

They exchanged troubled glances.

'I shall ring Mother later on this evening,' said Ruth, 'and we'll keep in touch about developments.'

A yell from across the road drew her attention to her daughter who was struggling to climb over the Hursts' gate.

'I must be off,' she said hastily, and dashed to the rescue.

Joan returned thoughtfully to the garden. Of course, as Ruth said, the parents were only coming for a short stay. But this was a reminder that the future must be faced.

When Edward came home they must have a serious talk about plans. They really must think of the years ahead.

The family cat met her at the door, and rubbed round her legs, mewing vociferously.

'Poor old puss! I've forgotten your lunch and tea,' said Joan remorsefully. 'It's all this thinking ahead that's done it.'

The cat led the way purposefully towards the kitchen. As far as he was concerned, the next meal was as far ahead as he was prepared to consider.

3 Prospective Lodgers

IF the Youngs' house was acknowledged to be the most beautiful at Thrush Green, the rectory, it was admitted ruefully, was the ugliest.

Unlike its neighbours, its Cotswold stone walls had been clad by some Victorian vandal in grey stucco. It was tall and bleak. It faced east rather than south, and the front door opened upon a long dark corridor which ran straight to the back door, thus creating a wind tunnel which worked so successfully that the unlucky dwellers there needed a fortune to keep the house warm.

Despite the fuel bills, the present inhabitants of the rectory were not unhappy. The Reverend Charles Henstock and his wife Dimity, considered themselves exceptionally lucky in their marriage, and in their work at Thrush Green. Material matters did not affect them greatly, and the fact that their home was cold, shabby, dark, and difficult to clean bothered Charles not at all, and Dimity only occasionally, and then mainly on her husband's behalf.

For years she had lived only some fifty yards from her present home, at a snug thatched cottage on the other side of the road. Her companion then had been a stalwart friend, called Ella Bembridge, who still lived there, and spent her spare time in creating textile designs, which she sometimes sold, and a great variety of handicrafts which she did not.

Not that these products were wasted. Ella's cupboards and drawers were stuffed with handwoven ties, raffia mats, cane basketwork, mirrors decorated with barbola work, wobbly teapot stands, and a number of unidentifiable objects, all of which were destined for Christmas presents or given to charitable institutions, preferably those concerned with animals. Ella rated the animal race rather more deserving than the human one, and who can blame her?

The cottage had been warm, Dimity was the first to admit. It faced south, and was sheltered by the hill which rose steeply from Lulling to Thrush Green. Furthermore, Ella enjoyed a fire, and never returned from her walks without some fire-wood or fir cones with which to create a cheerful blaze in the evenings. It was not until Dimity had spent her first winter at the rectory that she realised quite how bleak was her present abode.

'The trouble with this barn of a place,' said Ella one morning towards the end of April, 'is that it faces the wrong way. You get no sunshine at all, except in the kitchen. Frankly, I'd live in there.'

She thrust a bunch of daffodils at Dimity.

'Here, these should cheer things up a bit. They're some you planted years ago near the gooseberry bushes.'

'Thank you, dear. They are simply lovely. I shall put some on Charles's desk. The study does tend to be a little dark. Have some coffee?'

'Yes, please. I tried some jasmine tea yesterday that I'd dried myself, but can't say it's really palatable. Probably be better as potpourri. Pity to waste it.'

'You've heard about Mr Bassett, I suppose?' said Dimity, setting out cups upon a tray.

'No? Dead, is he?'

'No, no, Ella! I know he's been far from well, but he's nowhere near dead yet.'

'Sorry, sorry. What's the news then?'

'He's coming down for a rest after a rather nasty illness. Mrs Bassett too, of course.'

'Good. A nice pair. Might get a game of bridge. I miss dear old Donald Bailey for that.'

'I miss him for a lot of things,' replied Dimity. 'And so does Charles.'

At that moment, her husband entered, advanced upon Ella as though about to kiss her, remembered she did not like to be kissed, hastily stood up again, and contented himself with energetic hand-rubbing.

'Yes, they're due next week, I gather,' said Charles. 'But I'm afraid they'll miss the fair. A pity really. I always enjoy the Curdles' fair.'

'Not the same without the old lady,' said Ella, taking out a battered tin and beginning to roll one of the noisome cigarettes for which she was renowned. 'I like young Ben, but I shouldn't be a bit surprised if he didn't give up the job one day.'

'But he can't!' cried Dimity. 'Why, it's a sacred trust!'

'Not *sacred*, my dear,' corrected the rector mildly. 'He may have a *loyalty* to the business and to the memory of his grand-mother, but that's not quite the same thing.'

'Well, I can't imagine May the first at Thrush Green without the Curdles' fair blaring and gyrating for hours,' said Ella, putting a match to the ragged end of the very thin cigarette which drooped from her lips. 'But, come to think of it, why on earth should Ben Curdle want to give up a perfectly good living?'

'I very much doubt,' said Charles, pushing an ashtray towards his friend, 'if the fair really does bring in much these days. People demand rather more sophisticated pleasures than our forbears did. And of course there's television to contend with.'

At this moment, the milk rose with a joyous rush to the brim of the saucepan and was about to drench the stove, when Ella, with remarkable speed for one so bulky, leapt towards it, removed it from the heat, and blew heavily across its surface. The milk sank back obediently, and Dimity expressed her gratitude.

She did so with some inner misgivings. She could not feel that Ella's smoke-laden breath could be truly hygienic in contact with milk, but common civility forbade her from pouring it down the sink and starting again. Putting aside her qualms, she poured coffee for the three of them at the kitchen table.

'That smells good!' said Ella, sniffing greedily. 'I'm rationing myself with coffee since it's become so expensive. I did try ground acorns which Dotty said were almost as good, but I found them revolting.'

'Does Dotty really use ground acorns?' asked Charles. 'She hasn't offered me acorn coffee yet. At least, I don't think she has. I must admit that Dotty's coffee always tastes a little – well – er, peculiar.'

'Dear old Dotty is the prize eccentric of all time,' said Ella, 'and I love her dearly, but I try not to eat or drink anything of her making ever since I was laid up for three days with Dotty's Collywobbles after drinking her confounded elder-berry wine. D'you remember, Dim?'

'Indeed I do. It stained the kitchen sink a deep purple, I remember. One of Dotty's more potent brews.'

'To come upon Dotty at her cooking,' went on Ella, 'is rather like looking in on the three witches in Macbeth. You know, 'tongue of bat and leg of frog', or whatever it is. I certainly saw her fish a fat spider out of the milk jug before making a rice pudding. It's a wonder she doesn't suffer from her own creations.'

'Hardened to it, no doubt,' said Dimity.

'You are not being very charitable,' reproved the rector. 'Whatever her funny little ways, she has a heart of gold. I hear she has taken on a poor dog which some callous brute aban-doned at the side of the main road.'

'Good for Dotty!' cried Ella, 'but how will she manage? That place of hers is crammed with animals already. It must cost her a fortune in food for them. It beats me how she copes. I find it hard enough. In fact, I'm thinking of getting a lodger to help out.'

Her friends looked at her in amazement.

'Are you serious?'

'Well, nothing's definite yet, but there's your old room empty, Dimity, and it seems a shocking waste when the Third World is being rammed down your throat whenever you switch on the television. Besides, a few pounds a week would certainly help with the food bills. I haven't quite got to Dotty's stage of searching the hedgerows for my lunch.'

'Don't do anything too hastily,' warned Dimity. 'I mean,

you might get a dreadful man who turned out to be violent or dishonest – '

'Or a drunkard,' put in the rector, retrieving the ashtray, which had not been touched, and putting it resignedly on the windowsill again. Ella's saucer was holding the stub of the pungent cigarette, and ash sprinkled the table.

'Or simply someone with *designs* on you,' went on Dimity earnestly. 'There really are some terribly wicked men about. He might even make suggestions.'

'That'll be the day,' said Ella robustly. She stood up and dusted the rest of the ash to the floor.

'Don't worry. It may never come to pass, and in any case I don't want to be cluttered up with a man as a lodger. He'd want too much done – socks mended, shirts ironed, and all that razmatazz. No, a nice quiet woman is what I had in mind. Do for herself, and be no bother.'

'Well, just don't *rush* into anything,' pleaded Dimity. 'It's better to be poor and happily solitary, than rich with unpleasant company.'

Ella patted her friend's thin shoulder.

'I promise not to be rash. And now I must get back to the garden. You can't see my lettuce seedlings for groundsel.'

She vanished down the dark passage to the front door, and crossed the road to her own snug abode opposite.

Dotty Harmer lived about half a mile from Thrush Green, in a cottage which stood beside the track leading to Lulling Woods.

For years Dotty had kept house for her martinet of a father, a local schoolmaster, feared by generations of Thrush Green and Lulling boys for his iron discipline. On his death, Dotty had sold the house in Lulling and bought this secluded cottage where she lived very happily, quite alone, but for a varied menagerie ranging from goats to kittens.

Whilst Ella, Dimity and Charles were imbibing coffee Dotty was sitting on a fraying string stool in her hall, telephoning the local police station. At her feet lay a golden cocker spaniel, its eyes fixed trustingly upon her.

'Yes, yes,' Dotty was saying testily, 'I am quite aware that I gave you full particulars when I telephoned two days ago. The purpose of this call is to find out if there have been any more enquiries.'

There was the sound of rustling paper.

'Well, ma'am, there doesn't seem to be any message about a lost dog. A golden cocker, you said?'

He remembered that Dotty was unmarried, elderly and perhaps rather prim. He broached his next question with some delicacy.

'Would it be a lady or a gentleman?'

'It's a *bitch*, officer,' said Dotty, who spoke plain English. 'A bitch of about six months old, I should say. Rather thin, and with sore feet – obviously had travelled some way along the main road to Caxley. No collar, of course, but a very nice little dog.'

'Would you want us to take it – her, I mean – to the kennels for you, ma'am?'

'No, indeed. Excellent though I'm sure they are. No, the little thing has settled in very well since Friday, and I am quite prepared to adopt her if she is not claimed.'

'Thank you, ma'am. In that case, I'll make a note to that effect.'

'But, of course, you will telephone immediately if the owner comes forward? I should not wish to deprive anyone of their own animal, although I have the strongest suspicion that this one was purposely abandoned, in the most callous fashion. You are perhaps studying that side of this affair?'

'We're doing everything possible,' said the constable earnestly, eyeing a mug of tea which had been placed at his elbow by a fellow policeman. 'We'll let you know if anything comes of our enquiries.'

'Very well, officer, I shall let you return to your duties. I know how hard-pressed the force is.'

'Thank you, ma'am,' said the constable, replacing the receiver, with a sigh, and picking up the mug.

'Chuck over the paper, Ted,' he called to his colleague. 'Haven't had a minute to look at the headlines yet. All go, innit?'

Dotty replaced her receiver, and surveyed her new charge with affection.

'Good little Floss,' she said kindly. 'Good little dog.'

She was rewarded with a frantic lashing of Floss's fine plumy tail.

'It might be a good idea,' continued Dotty, rising from the disreputable stool, 'to give you a little walk today. On the grass, of course, with those tender feet. Perhaps a gentle stroll up to the green? We could take Ella's goat's milk to her, and save her a trip.'

She made her way into the kitchen, closely followed by the dog. A vast iron saucepan bubbled on the stove, cooking the hens' suppper. Floss looked at it hopefully, and barked.

'I think not, dear,' said Dotty, 'but I have a bone for you in the larder. Take it under the plum tree while I get ready.'

The bone was located under an old-fashioned gauze cover in the pantry. On the slate shelf beside it were a number of receptacles holding food suitable for Dotty's varied family – corn, bran mash, chopped lettuce leaves, crusts of bread, tinned cat food and the like. The provisions for Dotty seemed non-existent.

Dotty watched Floss gnawing the bone in the shady garden. A fine little animal! Very intelligent too, and very nice to have another Flossie after so many years.

She had been eight years old when she had been given the first Flossie as a birthday present. That little bitch had been another cocker spaniel, but black with mournful eyes, and a sweet and saintly expression which quite belied its destructive nature. Rugs, slippers, upholstery, and Dotty's beloved dolls all fell prey to those sharp teeth, but still the whole family forgave her, including Dotty's stern father.

She was named after a great aunt of Dotty's. Aunt Floss had been christened Florence, after the famous Florence Nightingale, but she lacked her namesake's vigour, and retired to her red plush sofa when she was a little over forty.

Dotty could remember being taken to see her on the family's visits to London. Aunt Flossie's house was in the Bayswater Road, a dark gloomy establishment, and the drawing-room where she lay in majesty seemed to be the most depressing room of all.

The heavy chenille curtains were always half drawn. They were edged with woollen bobbles, looking like the seed pods which dangled from the plane trees on the other side of the window.

Aunt Floss's legs were always covered by a tartan rug. Not that Aunt Floss ever used the word *legs*. 'My *extremities*,' she would say plaintively, 'are very susceptible to draughts.'

A bamboo table stood beside the sofa, laden with medicine bottles and pill boxes, a carafe of water and the latest novel from the lending library. The room reeked of camphor, and to the young Dotty, used to the Cotswold air of Lulling, the stuffiness of this apartment was unendurable.

Aunt Flossie had a long sad face, and wore her hair parted in the middle, and gathered into bunches of ringlets, rather in the style of Elizabeth Barrett Browning. She certainly had a spaniel-like appearance, and when Dotty's father, in a rare mood of frivolity, suggested 'Flossie' for the name of her birthday puppy, the family agreed with much hilarity. Aunt Flossie, of course, never met her namesake, and would have thought the whole thing most indecorous had she ever heard about it.

Armed with an old-fashioned metal milk can with a secure lid, and with Floss-the-second on a long lead, Dotty emerged into the sunshine, and into the meadow at the end of her garden.

The footpath lay across rich grass, used for grazing cattle most of the year. At the moment, the fields were empty, starred with daisies and a few early buttercups. Soon there would be sheets of golden flowers, thought Dotty happily, all ready to

> Gild gloriously the bare feet
> That run to bathe . . .

Rupert Brooke, thought Dotty, might be out of fashion at the moment, but he had supplied her with many felicitous phrases which had given her joy throughout her life. She remained grateful to him.

Floss padded ahead at the end of the lead, keeping to the grass, and pausing now and then to sniff at some particularly fascinating scent. In ten minutes they had reached Thrush Green, and Dotty sat down upon a bench, in order to change the milk can from one hand to the other, and to admire the glory of spring flowers in the gardens.

The hanging baskets outside the Two Pheasants won her

approval, and the bright mats of purple aubretia and golden alyssum hanging from the low stone walls. Through the gate of the Youngs' house she could see a mass of daffodils and narcissi under the trees, and a particularly beautiful copper-coloured japonica was in full bloom against Harold Shoosmith's house. Even Albert Piggott's cottage had a few bedraggled wallflowers close to his doorstep.

'A time of hope,' commented Dotty to Floss who was busy licking a paw. 'We must remember that, Flossie dear. Let's trust that it augurs well for us too.'

Refreshed by her brief rest, she collected milk can and dog again, and made her way to see her old friend Ella Bembridge.

4 April Rain

MEANWHILE, at Ealing, Robert Bassett's mood changed from stunned shock to querulous fury, and finally to philosophic resignation. Milly, his wife, bore all with patience.

'The firm won't automatically crumble, my dear, just because you are away from the office,' she told him. 'Frank knows the ropes as well as you do, and has always coped during the holidays perfectly well. That old saying about no one being indispensable is absolutely true, so just stop worrying.'

Frank Martell had been with the firm all his working life, starting as office boy at a wage of twenty shillings a week, and soon promoted to thirty shillings a week when Robert Bassett had seen the boy's capabilities. He was now a man in his mid-forties, quiet, conscientious and absolutely trustworthy. To Robert he was still 'young Frank' despite the sprinkling of grey hairs round his ears, and Robert found it difficult to have to face the fact that he would have to give him full responsibility for the business during his own absence.

He felt better about the whole affair after Frank had spent an afternoon by the bedside going through a file of letters and orders. His grasp of affairs surprised Robert. Frank had never said much, and Robert had always been too busy to realise quite how much Frank knew of the running of the firm. His quiet confidence reassured the invalid, and when Milly returned to the bedroom, after seeing Frank out, she found her husband breathing more easily and looking very much more relaxed.

'He's done you good,' she commented. 'You'll sleep better tonight.'

'I believe I shall,' agreed Robert.

Milly brought him an omelette at half-past seven, and for the first time since the onset of his illness he emptied his plate.

When she had gone, he lay back upon the pillows contentedly. The door was propped ajar, and darkness was beginning to fall. He felt as he had as a child, secure and cosseted, with the door left open for greater comfort, and access to grown-ups in case of emergency.

His gaze roamed over the shadowy room. How little, over the past years, he had noticed the familiar objects around him!

He looked now, with renewed awareness, at these old inanimate friends. There, on the dressing-table, stood the shabby oval leather box containing the two splendid hair-brushes which his father had given him on his twenty-first birthday. They were still in daily use, but had far less hair to cope with these days.

Nearby stood the photograph of Milly as he first saw her, hair parted demurely in the middle, eyes upraised soulfully, and never a hint of a double chin. To his mind, she was better looking now, plump and white-haired, her complexion as peach-like as when they first met, and the tranquillity, which had first attracted him, as constant as ever. He had been lucky in his marriage, and lucky to have two beautiful daughters.

On the wall opposite the bed hung a fine print of the Duomo

of Florence. They had spent their honeymoon in that city, staying at a quiet hotel which had once been an ancient family home, not far from the cathedral. They had always promised themselves a return visit to that golden city, but somehow it had never happened.

'If I get over this,' said Robert aloud, 'I'm damned if we don't do it. That's the worst of life. One is everlastingly putting things off until it's too late.'

He smoothed the patchwork bedspread. Here was another reminder of the past, for Milly and the two girls had made it together, before marriage had taken them away from home to Thrush Green. Robert had teased them, he remembered, about ever finishing it. They must have spent three winters on the thing, he thought, now tracing the bright hexagons of silk with a finger.

Most of the furniture had come from his own shop, but the bedside table had stood beside his parents' bed. He remembered it well, at the side of his widowed mother during her last long illness, laden with medicine bottles, books and letters, much as it looked now, he thought, with a mild feeling of shock. Well, it had served the generations loyally, and no doubt would continue to be used by his children and grand-children. There was something very comforting in this quality of permanence. It put into perspective the brief frailty of man compared with the solid works of his hands.

Yes, here, all around him stood the silent witnesses of his life. He was glad to have had this enforced breathing space to acknowledge his debt to faithful old friends.

He slid farther down the bed, sighing happily. When his wife came with hot milk at ten o'clock, she found him in a deep sleep, and crept away again, with a thankful heart.

The last few days of April brought torrential rain to Thrush Green. It drummed on the tarmac of the roads and the school playground, with relentless ferocity, so that it seemed as though a thousand silver coins spun upon the ground.

It cascaded down the steep Cotswold roofs, gurgled down the gutters, and a miniature river tossed and tumbled its way down the steep hill into Lulling High Street.

At the village school, rows of wellington boots lined the lobby, and mackintoshes dripped from the pegs. Playtimes were taken indoors. Dog-eared comics, incomplete and ancient jigsaw puzzles, and shabby packs of cards were in daily use, much to the children's disgust. They longed to be outside, yelling, running, leaping, fighting, and generally letting off steam, and would willingly have rushed there, despite the puddles and the downpour, if only their teachers had said the word.

Miss Fogerty, rearranging wet and steaming garments on the radiators, was thankful yet again for the comfort of her new classroom. At least her charges were able to pay their frequent visits to the lavatories under the same roof. In the old building it had been necessary to thread a child's arms into its mackintosh sleeves (invariably needing two or more attempts) before allowing it to cross the playground during a deluge. Really, thought Miss Fogerty, life was now very much simpler.

Next door to the village school, Harold Shoosmith, a middle-aged bachelor, struggled to locate a leak which had appeared in the back bedroom. He stood on a ladder, his head in the loft and a torch in his hand, while Betty Bell, his indefatigable daily help, stood below and offered advice.

'You watch out for bats, Mr Shoosmith! They was always partial to that loft. I remember as a girl the old lady as lived here then used to burn sulphur candles to get rid of them. Can you see any?'

'No,' came the muffled reply.

'You want a bucket for the drips?'

'No. I can't see a dam' thing.'

'You want another light? A candle, say?'

There was no answer, but Harold's trunk, then his thighs, and lastly his well-burnished brogues vanished through the trap-door, and thumps and shuffles proclaimed that the master of the house was surveying the highest point of his domain.

Betty Bell transferred her gaze from the gaping hole above her to the view from the streaming window. Rain slanted across the little valley at the back of the house, where Dotty Harmer's cottage glistened in the downpour. The distant Lulling Woods were veiled by rain, and the grey clouds, barely skimming the trees, told of more to come. She was going to have a wet ride home on her bike, that was sure.

'Found it!' came a triumphant call from above. 'It's running down one of the rafters. Get a thick towel, Betty, and a bucket, and I'll fix up a makeshift arrangement.'

'Right!' yelled Betty, 'and I'll put on your dinner. You'll need something hot after mucking about up there.'

She descended the stairs and caught a glimpse of a very wet Thrush Green through the fanlight of the front door.

Across the expanse of puddles Winnie Bailey was battling her way towards Lulling with her umbrella already dripping.

'Never ought to be out,' thought Betty. 'At her age, in this weather! She'll catch her death.'

But Winnie was quite enjoying herself. There was something very pleasant in splashing along under the shelter of Donald's old umbrella. It was very old, but a beautiful affair of heavy silk and whalebone, and a wide band of solid gold encircled the base of the handle. It was certainly far more protection from the rain than her own elegant umbrella, which was smaller and flatter, and which she resolved to keep-for ornament rather than use in future.

There were very few people about, she noticed, as she descended the hill to Lulling. Hardly surprising, in this weather, but what a lot they were missing! The stream of surface water gushed and gurgled at her side. Silver drops splashed from trees and shrubs, and a fresh breeze whipped the colour into her cheeks. It was an exhilarating morning, and she remembered how much she had loved a boisterous day when she was a child, running with arms thrown wide, mouth open, revelling in the buffeting of a rousing wind.

She was on her way now to visit three old friends, the Misses Lovelock, who lived in a fine house in the High Street. They were making plans for one of Lulling's many coffee mornings, and although Winnie tried to dodge as many of these occasions as she could, the proposed effort was for a cause very dear to her heart, and that of her late husband's, the protection of birds.

If the three sisters had been on the telephone, Winnie might have been tempted to ring up and excuse herself on such a wet morning, but she was glad that the Lovelocks considered a telephone in the house a gross extravagance. She would have missed this lovely walk, she told herself, as she approached their door.

The sisters were, in fact, very comfortably off, but they thoroughly enjoyed playing the part of poverty-stricken gentlewomen. Their house was full of furniture, porcelain and silver objects which would have made the gentlemen at Sotheby's and Christie's pink with excitement. A great many of these exquisite items had been begged for by the mercenary old ladies who had brought the art of acquiring other people's property, for nothing or almost nothing, to perfection. They were a byword in Lulling, and newcomers were warned in advance, by those luckless people who had succumbed in a weak moment to the sisters' barefaced blandishments.

Winnie had been invited to coffee, and was quite prepared for the watery brew and the one Marie biscuit which would be presented to her on a Georgian silver tray.

She was divested of her streaming mackintosh and umbrella in the hall, the Misses Lovelock emitting cries of horror at her condition.

'So brave of you, Winnie dear, but *reckless*. You really shouldn't have set out.'

'You must come into the drawing-room at once. We have *one bar* on, so you will dry very nicely.'

Miss Bertha stroked the wet umbrella appreciatively as she deposited it in a superb Chinese vase which did duty as an umbrella stand in the hall. There was a predatory gleam in her eye which did not escape Winnie.

'What a magnificent umbrella, Winnie dear! Would that

be *gold*, that exquisite band? I don't recall seeing you with it before.'

'It was Donald's. It was so wet this morning I thought it would protect my shoulders better than my own modern thing. As you can guess, I treasure it very much.'

'Of course, of course,' murmured Bertha, removing her hand reluctantly from the rich folds. 'Dear Donald! How we all miss him.'

The ritual of weak coffee and Marie biscuit over, the silver tray and Sèvres porcelain were removed and the ladies took out notebooks and pencils to make their plans.

'We thought a Bring and Buy stall would be best for raising money,' explained Violet. 'We can use the dining-room, and Bertha took a lot of geranium and fuchsia cuttings last autumn

which should sell well, and Ada has made scores of lavender bags from a very pretty organdie blouse which was our dear mother's.'

'Splendid,' said Winnie, stifling the unworthy thought that these offerings would not have cost her old friends a penny.

'And Violet,' chirped Ada proudly, 'has made dozens of shopping lists and jotters from old scraps of paper and last year's Christmas cards. They really are *most* artistic.'

Violet smiled modestly at this sisterly tribute.

'And we thought we might ask Ella for some of her craft work. She has managed to collect a variety of things, I know, over the years. Would you like to ask her to contribute? It would save us calling in.'

'Of course,' said Winnie, 'and Jenny and I will supply all the home-made biscuits to go with the coffee, if that suits you.'

The Misses Lovelock set up a chorus of delight. Pencils moved swiftly over home-made notebooks and all was joy, and comparative warmth, within, as the rain continued to pelt down outside.

Albert Piggott, standing in the church porch with a sack draped, cowl-wise over his head, gazed at the slanting rain with venom.

He took the downpour as a personal affront. Here he was, an aging man with a delicate chest, obliged to make his way through that deluge to his own door opposite. And he had a hole in the sole of his shoe.

When Nelly had looked after him, he thought, she had

always kept an eye on such things. She'd washed his shirts, brushed the mud off his trouser legs, darned his socks, sewn on all them dratted buttons that burst off a chap's clothes, and took his shoes down to Lulling to be mended when the time came.

No doubt about it, Nelly had had her uses, hussy though she turned out to be.

'I bet that oil man's found out his mistake by now,' said Albert to a spider dangling from a poster exhorting parishioners of Thrush Green to remember their less fortunate fellows in darkest Africa.

He hitched the sack more firmly round his shoulders, and made a bolt across the road. Which should it be? Home, or the Two Pheasants? The latter, of course, won.

'Lord, Albert, you're fair sopped!' cried the landlord. 'Been digging up the graves or something?'

Albert ignored the facetious remark, and the titters of the regulars.

'Half a pint of the usual,' he grunted, 'and I wouldn't mind a look at the fire, if it ain't asking too much of you gentlemen.'

The little knot of customers, steaming comfortably by the blaze, moved a short distance away, allowing Albert to enter the circle.

'Terrible weather,' said one, trying to make amends for any offence given.

Albert maintained a glum silence.

'Bashing down the daffodils,' said another. 'Pity really.'

Albert took a swig at his beer. He might have been an aging carthorse taking a drink at the village pond for all the noise he made. The customers avoided each other's eyes.

'You getting your own dinner, Albert, or d'you want a hot pie here?' asked the landlord.

'How much?'

'Same as usual. And as good as your Nelly ever made, I'm telling you.'

Albert cast him a sharp look.

'There's no call to bring my wife into it. But I'll have a pie all the same, daylight robbery though it is, you chargin' that amount!'

'*Daisy*,' shouted the landlord through an inner door. 'Hot pie for Albert, toot-der-sweet.'

Uneasy silence fell upon all as Albert waited, mug in hand. A sudden gust of wind shook the door, and a little trickle of rainwater began to seep below it and run down the step into the bar.

'Blimey!' said one of the men, 'we're goin' to be flooded out.'

'Can't go on much longer,' said his companion, retrieving the doormat before it became soaked. 'Rain this heavy never lasts long.'

'It's been on for two days,' remarked Albert, accepting his hot pie, 'don't see no sign of it letting up either.'

The landlord bustled forward with a mop and bucket.

'Here, stand away and I'll clear up.'

He began to attack the rivulet.

'Let's hope it stops before the month's out,' he puffed, wielding the mop energetically. 'Be a pity if Curdle's Fair gets this sort of weather.'

'Always gets a change afore the beginning of May,' announced one aged regular in the corner.

'You mark my words now.' He raised a trembling fore-finger. 'I never knowed old Mrs Curdle have a wet day at Thrush Green. We'll get a fine day for the fair, that I knows. You just mark my words!'

'S'pose he's forgot the old lady died years ago,' whispered one customer to his neighbour.

'No, I ain't forgot!' rapped out the old man. 'And I ain't forgot as young Ben runs it now, and pretty near as good as his grandma.'

The landlord shouldered his mop and picked up the bucket.

'Shan't see you in here next week for hot pies then, Albert. I s'pose your young Molly will be cooking your dinner for you while the fair's here?'

Albert thrust the last of his pie into his mouth, and turned towards the door.

'Ever heard of mindin' your own business?' he asked sourly. 'First me wife, and now me daughter. You talks too much, that's your trouble.'

He opened the door, and a spatter of rain blew into the room. The newly dammed river gushed joyfully over the step again, and Albert departed.

'That miserable old devil was *grinning*!' said the landlord, and went into action once more, sighing heavily.

5 The Coming of Curdle's Fair

THE rain was still lashing down on the last day of April, as Ben Curdle and his wife Molly, *née* Piggott, approached Thrush Green with the fair.

They were a cheerful young couple, happy in their marriage, and proud of their little boy George, who was now four years of age.

The child sat between them as they towed their caravan at a sedate pace through the streaming countryside. Molly's spirits were high for she was returning home, and although Albert Piggott was never a particularly welcoming father, yet she looked forward to seeing him and the cottage where she had been born.

She was well aware that she would have to set to and do a great deal of scrubbing and general cleaning before the little house was fit for them all to live in for their few days' stay, but she was young and energetic and had never feared hard work.

She was looking forward too, to seeing the Youngs again. She had worked in their beautiful house for several years, before going to the Drovers' Arms where Ben Curdle had come a-courting. Joan Young had been a great influence and a good friend to the motherless young girl, and had taken pleasure in training such a bright and willing pupil in the ways of housewifery.

Molly had also acted as nursemaid to Paul Young when he was a baby, and had treasured the postcards and letters which the boy, now at school, sent from time to time. The happiest of her memories of Thrush Green were centred on that house, and working for the Youngs had been the highlight of her life. They had provided a haven from the dismal cottage across the green, and from the continuous complaining of her sour old father.

Ben Curdle's spirits were not quite so high. For one thing, he disliked his father-in-law, and resented the fact that his wife would have to work so hard in getting the neglected house together. But he was a sensible young fellow, and kept his feelings to himself. It was good to see Molly so happy, and he was wise enough to make sure that she remained so.

But he had another cause for worry. The fair was bringing in far less than when his redoubtable old grandmother had run it. Now that petrol and diesel oil had supplanted the shaggy-hoofed horses of her day, the cost of moving the fair from one place to the next was considerable. Takings too were down.

It was not only the counter-attraction of television in almost every home. That was one factor, of course, and who could blame people for staying comfortably under their own roofs, especially when the weather was as foul as it was today? No, it went deeper than that, Ben realised.

The fact was that most people wanted more sophisticated entertainment. The children still flocked to the fair, accompanied by adults. But the number of people who came without children was dwindling fast. In his grandmother's time, every-one virtually attended the great Mrs Curdle's Fair. It was something to which farmers, shop-keepers, school teachers, as well as their pupils, looked forward from one Mayday to the next. Those grown-ups came no more, unless it was to bring their children or grandchildren for an hour's frolic.

And then, his fair was so small, and likely to get smaller as the machinery wore out, for replacements were becoming prohibitively expensive. Ben himself was a good mechanic, and conscientious about keeping everything in apple-pie order, but as parts became worn and more and more difficult and costly to replace, he saw clearly that some of the attractions would have to be withdrawn. As it was, the famous switch-back, which had delighted so many generations at Thrush Green, would not be erected on this Mayday. It was altogether too shaky, and Ben was not the sort of man to take chances.

The thing was, what should he do? He was used to travelling the country and sometimes wondered if he could ever settle down in one place, even if he should be fortunate enough to find a congenial job.

And then, he was devoted to the fair and had never known any other way of living. His grandmother he had adored. She had brought him up from early childhood, for his father had been killed and his mother had married again. The old lady's upright and staunch principles had been instilled into this much-loved grandchild, and Ben had repaid her care with loyalty and respect. Not a day passed but he remembered some word of advice or some cheerful tag of his grand-mother's, and to give up the fair, which she had built up so laboriously, smacked of treachery to the young man.

But there it was. Something would have to be done, and soon. He turned his mind to an offer which had been made to him some weeks earlier, by the owner of a much larger concern.

This man had three large fairs touring the country. Over the years he had bought up many a small business, such as Ben's, and combined them into a highly-efficient organisation. He was astute, and could foresee possibilities which a slower man would not. He was not liked, for there was a strain of ruthlessness in him without which he could not have succeeded, but there was grudging respect for his ability, and it was agreed that he treated fairly those whom he employed, as long as they worked well.

Ben felt pretty sure that he would be offered a job if he decided to sell. But would he like working for a master after being his own for so long? And what about his fellow workers? He had little respect for some who had sold up and gone to work for Dick Hasler, and he had heard of some underhand transactions which disgusted him. No, if he had to make the break, it would be a clean one, and he would have a complete change. Surely, there must be something he could do to earn a living? His old grandmother always said he had the most useful pair of hands in the business. What honest living could he earn with them? Perhaps a job in a garage somewhere? He brooded silently, as windscreen wipers flashed to and fro hardly keeping pace with the torrent.

'Soon be there,' cried Molly. 'Look out for the river, Georgie! Once we're over that we're nearly home.'

Ben watched their excitement with a smile. So far he had said very little about the fair's diminishing profits, but Molly must have some inkling, and the time would soon come when they would be obliged to have a straight talk about the future.

The steep hill to Thrush Green was just ahead. Ben sighed, and changed gear. Slowly they came abreast of St Andrew's church, and drew to a halt outside Albert Piggott's cottage. From the joy which lit Molly's face, you might think it was Buckingham Palace, thought Ben wryly.

'Here we are,' she cried, 'home again!'

Ella Bembridge saw the Curdles arrive from her bedroom window. She had gone upstairs to rummage through drawers and cupboards to find some contributions to the Lovelocks' Bring and Buy stall, and Dimity was with her.

'They'll have to look slippy if they want the fair to be ready by the morning,' commented Ella. 'Don't envy them that job in this weather.'

'What about this cushion cover?' enquired Dimity, holding up a square of hessian embroidered in thick wool.

'It's a peg bag,' said Ella. 'Rather fine, isn't it? Bold, you know. Plenty of pure bright colour.'

She looked at the enormous flowers of scarlet and gold with affection.

'Too good for a Bring and Buy. Put it back, Dim. It'll do for a Christmas present.'

'What are they, dear?' Dimity was studying the blossoms, with some distaste. 'Zinnia? Red hot pokers? I can't quite recognise them.'

Ella gave her booming laugh.

'They're no known species. I just made 'em up as I went

along. You know, three threads up, four down, and all that.
Effective, isn't it?'

'Very,' said Dimity, folding the object carefully and returning it to the drawer.

'Here, they can have this magnolia talcum powder. I'll never
use that. Can't think who thought I'd relish magnolia scent.
Do I *look* like magnolia?'

'Well, no, Ella. Not really.'

'And this useless handkerchief sachet, and this idiotic comb
case. Here they come.'

Ella was now ferreting in the drawer like some eager fox
terrier in a rabbit hole. Objects flew from her towards the bed,
and Dimity did her best to sort them out.

'But Winnie said they wanted things you'd made,' she
pointed out, fielding a crocheted bobble cap rather neatly.

'They can have these as well,' replied Ella, head well
down. A long string of plastic beads, pretending to be
jet, swung through the air, Dimity added it to the motley
collection.

'Right,' said Ella, slamming the drawer back. 'Now let's
look in the cupboard.'

One turn of the handle burst open the door. Out from the
depths sprang a snarl of cane and raffia, and a few objects made
from similar material. Ella bent to retrieve them.

'Two waste paper baskets, and three bread roll holders!
What about that?'

'Lovely,' said Dimity faintly.

Ella looked at her handiwork approvingly.

'I was thinking of decorating them with raffia flowers,' she
mused. 'But what d'you think?'

'They are just right as they are,' replied Dimity firmly. 'No need to gild the lily, you know.'

'Yes, you're right. Somewhere at the back there are some teapot stands. Push over the chair, Dim, and I'll have a look.'

She clambered up with surprising agility for one of her bulk, and began to scrabble at the back of a high shelf. Dimity drifted to the window and looked out at rain-washed Thrush Green.

Ben Curdle was carrying a large suitcase into Albert Piggott's cottage, and young George was capering beside him, glorying in the puddles.

'Got 'em!' came Ella's triumphant call. 'Catch!'

Dimity caught about half a dozen wooden teapot stands, edged with cane and beadwork, wrapped in a polythene bag, and added them to the pile.

'There!' said Ella, stepping down heavily. 'That's a pretty good haul, isn't it? Do them a good turn, and me too, come to think of it. If I ever take a lodger I shall have to clear out all the shelves and drawers in this room. Made a start anyway.'

'So you're still thinking about it?' said Dimity, following her old friend downstairs.

'Oh, I honestly don't know,' replied Ella, settling in a chair and fishing in her pocket for the battered tobacco tin which contained her cigarette factory. She began to roll one of her deplorable cigarettes. She looked pensive.

'It's like this,' she began, blowing out a cloud of acrid smoke. 'I can do with the money and I've got plenty of spare room, but I'm wondering if I should find a lodger congenial.'

'Anyone in mind?'

'Not really, although I believe Winnie Bailey's nephew Richard is looking for somewhere to stay, but no doubt Winnie would put him up.'

'Are you going to advertise?'

'I think not. I've decided to see if I hear of anyone – personal recommendation, that sort of thing. I don't want a stream of folk banging at the door.'

'Well, I must say I'm relieved to know you are not doing anything too hastily. I know Charles has mentioned it in his prayers.'

Ella patted Dimity's thin arm gratefully.

'You're a good pair. It's plain to see your religion is the mainspring of your lives. Lucky old you!'

'It could be yours too.'

Ella shook her head sadly.

'You know me, Dim. Full of honest doubts. Whenever I read "Thanks to St Jude" in the personal column I think: "How do they know St Jude reads this paper?" It's no good, I'm afraid. What I can't see I can't believe in. I suppose you find that pathetic?'

'Not at all. Someone as honest as you are is never pathetic. But I grieve for all you are missing. If you are a believer then you have so much to look forward to.'

'Bully for you,' said Ella cheerfully, 'but time alone will tell. Here, let's brew a cup of something, and let the future look after itself.'

Within an hour of his arrival, Ben and his workmates were hard at it erecting the various attractions of Curdle's Fair. A knot of interested spectators had assembled, and at playtime the railings of the village school were thick with pupils eager to see what was afoot.

Little Miss Fogerty, patrolling the wet playground, but thankful for a clearing sky at last, determined to make 'The Fair' a subject for the afternoon session, and only hoped that she had enough paper to supply the class with adequate artistic material.

Joan Young, making up beds in the room intended for her parents, noted the preparations outside with approval. Still more encouraging were the patches of blue sky which were appearing over Lulling Woods, and the gentle movement of low clouds moving away to the east, and giving way to high ones from the west. It certainly looked as though the fair would have its usual fine weather.

She smoothed the bedspreads and then went to the window. Leaning out she felt the soft breeze lift her hair. The avenue of chestnut trees still shed an occasional drop into the puddles below, and their stout trunks were striped with little rivulets of water, but there was a warmth in the air which spoke of better weather to come.

The daffodils and narcissi, which had taken such a battering in the last few days, were beginning to lift their heads again, and the wallflowers, their velvety faces still wet, were giving out a heady fragrance.

Tight buds beaded the cherry tree nearby, and soon would burst into dangling snow, and the lilac bushes, massed with pyramids of buds, would soon be adding their perfume.

Tomorrow was May. Ever since she could remember, May the first had meant the coming of Curdle's Fair and the real beginning of summer. Her spirits always rose with the advent of May, 'loveliest of months', as the poet truly said.

Even now, she thought, with a great many problems ahead, her heart leapt to greet the fair, the flowers, the coming of summer, and the knowledge that Thrush Green would soon be gilded with sunshine, and aflutter with birds and butterflies.

It was good to know that her father would be with them at the most beautiful time of the year. Thrush Green could not fail to restore him to health. Of that she felt positive, as she ran downstairs full of hope.

By the time the children ran home from school, a watery sun was shining, sparkling upon the drying roofs and the wet grass of Thrush Green.

The air was filled with the clashing of hammers on metal, and the thump of mallets on wood, as the massive equipment of the fair was assembled.

Ben walked purposefully from one site to the next, followed by the diminutive figure of young George clad in duffle coat and wellingtons. He was a sensible child, and obedient to his father's directions. He knew that if he did not do as he was told, and keep out of harm's way, then he would be dispatched back to his mother without further ado.

Back at the cottage, Molly was making a cup of tea for Albert. She had scrubbed the kitchen table, the draining-board and the cupboard tops, and thrown away several revolting remnants of food in various crocks and saucepans.

After the teabreak she resolved that she would get her father to depart across the road to his church duties, while she had an energetic session with soap, hot water and the scrubbingbrush on the filthy kitchen floor.

There was no doubt about it, Albert Piggott's standards of cleanliness grew lower and lower as the years passed.

She looked across at him now, as he sat sipping his tea noisily. It was not just the house which he neglected. The man himself looked half-starved, sickly and dirty. Molly's kind heart was stirred. He had never been a good father, but after all, blood was thicker than water, and she wanted to see him in better shape than this.

It was a pity that Nelly, her stepmother, had ever left him, although she could not blame her. Admittedly, Nelly was avaricious, flighty and coarse. Nevertheless, she was warm-hearted and lively, and the little cottage had never been so clean and wholesome as when Nelly had cared for it. And Albert had always looked spruce and well-fed, his linen spotless, his shoes polished. He looked now, thought Molly, as if he needed a thorough scrubbing and a completely new set of clothing from top to toe.

'I'd best take me tablets with me tea,' said Albert, rising to run a hand along the mantelpiece. The movement triggered off a vicious bout of coughing.

Molly watched with alarm as the old man rested his forehead on the shelf, his thin frame racked with the cough. It ended at last, and Albert sat down again, medicine phial in hand, and drew great noisy breaths.

'You didn't ought to be about, Dad,' said Molly earnestly, 'with that chest of yours. What about havin' a day in bed? I could ask Doctor Lovell to come and see you.'

'He's seen me,' retorted Albert, 'and a fat lot of good that be! If I takes these tablets it do seem to help a bit.'

He rammed one in his mouth, and sent it down his throat with a mouthful of tea.

'What you want,' went on Molly, 'is a good hot bath. The steam'd do them tubes good, you know. Then a day or two resting in bed. You're properly knocked up, and I don't believe you ever feed yourself, do you?'

'I gets a hot pie next door when I'm clemmed,' muttered Albert.

'And plenty of drink to go with it, I don't doubt,' remarked Molly with spirit. 'And that don't do you a ha'porth of good. You could do with a regular dosing of Nelly's cooking.'

'And you could do with minding your own business,' said Albert nastily. 'I manages all right, and I won't have that trollop crossing my doorstep again.'

He rose shakily, and took down his deplorable jacket and cap from the peg on the door.

'Best see to the church, I suppose, while I've got me strength.'

He slammed the door behind him. Molly shook her head sadly and filled the kettle again, ready for her onslaught on the kitchen floor.

It was all very well for him to tell her to mind her own business. As a daughter, his welfare *was* her business. If he went on as he was at present, he would very soon find himself back in hospital, or in one of Lulling's almshouses. The thought of either filled Molly's mind with horror.

She was half inclined to try to get in touch with Nelly. After all, legally she was his wife, even if she had left him for the charms of the oil man.

On the other hand, Albert had every right to refuse to have her back. It was his house. She had treated him shabbily, and no doubt the two would fight like cat and dog, if they were ever brought together again.

Lord, what a to-do it all was, thought Molly! She would have to see what Ben could do about it.

Perhaps he could persuade her father to have at least one decent meal a day. Someone might come in to cook it, or the Two Pheasants might provide it regularly. They could leave the landlord some money in advance.

Meanwhile, she determined that her father was going to be got into a bath, by hook or by crook, and she would burn those filthy clothes herself, and face the storm afterwards.

Much refreshed by these brave plans, she attacked the kitchen floor, and rejoiced in the shadowy pattern on the linoleum which gradually reappeared as the result of her energy.

6 The First of May

MAY the first fell on a Thursday, and it was Ben's intention to stay at Thrush Green until the middle of the following week. Most of his takings would come on Friday night and Saturday. He might pick up enough to cover expenses early in the following week, if the weather held, but he was not due at his next stand for a full week, and he wanted Molly to have time to see all her Thrush Green friends and to get her father's domestic arrangements straightened out.

Not that they could do anything to satisfy that curmudgeonly old fellow, Ben realised. He was a real problem, and likely to become worse as the years passed. He disliked the idea of living near the old man, and yet he had begun to wonder if that might have to be, as his father-in-law's health failed. Of one thing he was quite positive—he would never live under the same roof with him. It was bad enough to watch Molly wearing herself out, once or twice a year. To see her slaving for that old tyrant, day in and day out, would be impossible, and he was not going to stand for that, whatever the future held.

The day of the fair dawned with a respite from the rain, but no one could truthfully call it 'Mrs Curdle's weather'. The old lady had always seemed to bring sunshine and cloud-

less skies, but this particular morning was overcast, with only a
few shreds of blue sky among the grey mass to give hope of
better things to come.

During the day, Ben completed the preparations to his
satisfaction, and gave the men an hour or two off. The fair
would open at four o'clock, and most of the trade would come
from mothers with young children, for the first two or three
hours.

After that, with any luck, a good crowd of adults would
arrive, willing to spend and out to enjoy some boisterous fun.
At ten-thirty the fair must close, so that Ben earnestly hoped
that the rain would hold off for the next few days, and particularly during those few vital hours each day when he hoped
to recoup some of his outlay.

He was determined to try and get Molly alone for an hour
during the afternoon, out of earshot of her father, and to tell
her a little about his fears for the future of the fair. Not that
she was completely ignorant of its diminishing returns. It was
she who kept the rudimentary accounts, and she who helped
at one of the stalls whenever she could. It did not need a vast
intelligence to see that the crowds were thinner than before,
and that takings were down, but Ben feared that she did not
realise how dangerously low their resources were. She knew
nothing of the offer made by Dick Hasler, and Ben wanted to
know how she felt about it.

A fine brown steak and kidney pie dominated the table
at midday, and they all did justice to Molly's cooking. Even
the old man, Ben noticed, tucked in, and grunted his apprecia-
tion in a grudging fashion.

'Now, you go and have a lay down, Dad,' said kindly Molly

'while we wash up. Do you good to have a nap, and I'll wake you in time to go over to the church.'

Albert departed aloft and the young couple went to the sink. George was busy with his bricks at the table before going for his own brief rest. Now, thought Ben, was the time to broach the delicate subject. But Molly forestalled him.

'How d'you think dad seems?'

'Not too bad. Ate two platefuls of pie, so he can't be at death's door yet. You worry overmuch about him, and he plays up to you.'

'That's not wholly true. His breathing's that rattly it scares me. He'll be back in hospital if he don't take care, and he's no more likely to do that than young George there.'

'He's a grown man. You can't expect to do everything for him.'

'And that ain't all,' went on Molly. 'His underclothes is in rags. I've torn up most of 'em for dusters as I've washed 'em, and I've taken a set of yours for him to keep the old fellow going until I can get down to Lulling to set him up.'

'Thanks,' said Ben laconically. 'And who pays for the new clobber?'

'Well, he will. I'll see to that. He's got a bit put by in the Post Office, and it's time he took some out for a few decent warm clothes. He don't know yet, but I had a bonfire of some of the worst this morning.'

Ben looked startled, and nearly dropped the pie-dish he was wiping.

'Watch it, girl!' he cried. 'He can be real nasty when he's roused. Lord knows the sparks'll fly when he finds out.'

'Then they must fly,' said Molly flatly, tipping away the

washing-up water. 'I'm going to sort him out before we move on next week. And what's more, he's going to be given a good hot bath tonight, come what may!'

'Well, you can face that fight while I'm over the fair,' said Ben. 'And good luck to you!'

He watched her militant face as she shepherded George upstairs for his rest. This was not the time, he thought sadly, to introduce the subject of their own troubles.

That would have to wait.

Harold Shoosmith was busy weeding among the wallflowers by his front gate.

He viewed the fair with mixed feelings. A peace-loving man who had retired to Thrush Green because of its tranquillity, he personally loathed the noise which Curdle's Fair generated, and for that reason would rejoice when the great trailers and caravans departed, leaving the green to recover from the scars.

On the other hand, he was amused and impressed by the ardour with which almost all the older inhabitants greeted May the first. The rites of spring had nothing on it, thought Harold, removing a worm which had become entangled in his shoe-lace. He dropped it nearby, and was roundly scolded by a robin who had been looking forward to snapping up this delectable morsel, but did not dare to come too close.

It was natural that the children should be excited, but surprising to find Joan Young and her sister Ruth Lovell so exhilarated at the thought of going on the swingboats and roundabouts as though they were still about ten years old. Even dear old Charles Henstock had rubbed his hands gleefully, and had said how good it was to see the fair again.

He straightened his creaking back and observed Phyllida Hurst coming out of her gate, across the green, letter in hand.

He waved to her and she waved back, and after putting the envelope in the pillar box at the corner of the green, she walked over to talk to him.

She grew prettier than ever, thought Harold. There had been a time when he had fancied himself in love with this attractive young widow, but she had married his good friend Frank and, on the whole, he was relieved to find himself still a bachelor. But now and again he had a twinge of regret. It must be very comforting to come home to find a pretty woman there, to have someone to talk to, to laugh with, and to share one's problems.

'That's exactly what I should be doing,' observed Phil, pointing a toe at the bucket of weeds, 'but I had a horrible story to alter this morning, and it's put me back in the day's programme.'

'How's the writing going?'

'Oh, slowly. I've about four or five magazines who take stuff regularly, but I'm thankful to say I don't have to worry so dreadfully about making money.'

'I'm very glad to hear it,' said Harold. 'You've quite enough to keep you happily occupied, and that's what matters.'

'Are you going to the fair?'

Harold noticed that the girl's eyes were sparkling as brightly as Joan's and Ruth's.

'Well, no! I'm a bit long in the tooth for all that whizzing round.'

'Rubbish!' said Phil. 'It does your liver a world of good!

I'm taking Jeremy as soon as he comes out of school, and if Frank gets home in time, I hope I can persuade him to come too later on.'

'You'll manage that,' Harold told her with conviction.

She laughed, and moved away.

'Change your mind,' she called. 'Do come if you can. It's tremendous fun.'

He smiled, but made no reply. He had no intention of getting mixed up with a noisy, shouting throng of people, of being deafened with the brazen notes from those dreadful hurdy-gurdys, and of tripping over coils of cable on the wet grass of Thrush Green.

But how easy it would have been to say 'Yes' to that invitation.

Lucky Frank, thought Harold, turning again to his digging.

Promptly at four o'clock the strident music of Curdle's Fair rent the air. Outside the booths stood the showmen, shouting their wares. The swingboats began their delectable movement up and down, and the galloping horses moved steadily round and round and up and down, their barley-sugar brass supports gleaming like gold.

Most of the patrons were the children from the village school, with a few mothers. Jeremy, in company with some schoolfellows and his mother, Phil, was astride the horses and ostriches within five minutes of the fair's opening. If all his customers were as thrilled as this small boy, thought Ben, then this year's visit to Thrush Green might be well worth while.

His thoughts flew back to his wonderful old grandmother whose grave was behind him in the churchyard. She had always looked upon Thrush Green as her true home, the one place where she felt that she could rest, largely because of the affection she felt for Dr Bailey, who had looked after her, so many years ago, at her confinement with George, her son, father to Ben.

Ben too had this feeling of affinity with Thrush Green, partly because of his grandmother's loyalty to the place, partly because she now rested there for ever, and partly, of course, because he had found his dear Molly here, and heard about it from her almost daily, wherever they happened to be.

Yes, he supposed Thrush Green would be the obvious place

to settle if the fair had to go. He sighed at the thought. What would the old lady have said?

Guilt flooded him, but within a minute it had given way to a comforting thought. Mrs Curdle had always been a realist. If one stall did not pay its way, she was quite ruthless in scrapping it.

When she had discovered her nephew Sam stealing the takings, she had not hesitated to banish him from the fair. If now she had been alive and had to face the sad fact that the business was not thriving, she would do as Ben was thinking of doing, cut her losses and start afresh, with courage and a stout heart.

It was a warming thought, and Ben felt better as he watched the spinning roundabout and the gaudy booths. She would have understood, and so would Molly when he broke the news.

'Roll up! Roll up!' he shouted with vigour, hoisting a four-year-old into a swingboat, and setting it into movement with a cheerful shove.

Some hours later, Winnie Bailey surveyed the scene from her bedroom window. By now it was dark. A few stars pricked the clearing sky, but it was difficult to see them against the blaze of light from Curdle's Fair.

'It's even better at night,' Winnie murmured to herself, watching the moving figures silhouetted against the glare of the bright lamps. She had a great affection for the fair. The bond between Mrs Curdle, of hallowed memory, and Donald and herself had endured for decades. Every year the old lady had made a magnificent bouquet of artificial flowers for her

Thrush Green friends. If she had kept them all, thought Winnie, she must have had several dozen.

They were glowing gaudy blossoms, made of finely-pared wood, and dyed in bright shades of orange, pink and red. Winnie still had one of these offerings in a vase on the landing, a constant reminder of a faithful friend.

'A fine family,' commented Winnie, closing the window.

Tomorrow she would seek out Ben and Molly, and hear all their news. The girl must enjoy coming home again and seeing Albert.

As it happened, at that very moment, Molly was confronting her incensed father across a zinc bath half full of steaming water.

The kitchen was snug and steamy. The kitchen range was alight, and on its gleaming top stood a large kettle and the biggest saucepan the cottage could boast.

'Never!' shouted Albert, his face suffused with wrath. 'I ain't gettin' in there, and that's flat.'

'You are,' replied Molly. 'You're plain filthy. You smell somethin' chronic, and you can get them rags off of your back for me to wash, or burn maybe, and get soaping. I'll be upstairs, sorting George's things out, so nobody's going to stare at you.'

'Never!' shouted Albert again. 'Never 'eard such cheek!'

Molly looked at him grimly.

'D'you want me to get the *District Nurse*?'

Albert's bravado cracked a little.

'You wouldn't dare! Besides, it's not decent. That young woman? Why, she ain't even married!'

'She's coming tomorrow, if you don't do as I says, and we'll both get you into the tub. So take your choice.'

Slowly the old man fumbled with the greasy scarf about his scrawny neck. He was muttering crossly to himself.

'That's right,' said Molly, reaching for the kettle. 'I'll just top up the water, and you can have a good soak in front of the fire. See here, I'll spread the towel over the back of the chair. Warm it nice, that will, and keep the draught off of you.'

Her ministrations done, she mounted aloft, leaving the staircase door ajar in order to hear that the old man attended properly to his ablutions. Once he was in, she intended to return to scrub his neglected back, modesty or not. Heaven alone knew when Albert's body had last seen soap and water! Not since his last trip to hospital, Molly suspected.

Albert stepped out of the last of his dilapidated underwear. He put one toe reluctantly into the steaming water.

'Women!' muttered Albert, and braced himself for semi-immersion.

7 New Hopes

AS Miss Fogerty was on her way to school on Monday morning, she espied Willie Bond, the postman, pedalling towards her.

She waited at the end of the chestnut avenue. Willie was fat, and never hurried. However, Miss Fogerty was in good time, as usual, and observed while she waited, the fine sticky buds of the chestnut trees which were beginning to put forth little green fans of leaves.

'Morning, miss,' puffed Willie, dismounting. He studied a handful of letters and handed over two, much to Miss Fogerty's delight. She did not expect to get more than one or two in a whole week. Two in one day was quite an excitement.

She thanked Willie, and turned right between the trees, opening her first letter. It was a printed message from Messrs Ames and Barlow who, so their heading said, were Drapers, Milliners and Mantle Makers of 82 Lulling High Street, established 1862. They thanked Miss Fogerty for her esteemed order, and begged to inform her that the goods awaited collection at her earliest convenience, and they remained her obedient servants.

Miss Fogerty felt a little glow of pleasure. Her new light-weight mackintosh, ordered at Easter, would be a very welcome addition to her modest wardrobe. She might need to withdraw some money from her Post Office account, but it was a comfort to think that she could face the expense.

The other letter was from her dear friend Isobel, and she resolved to read it at her leisure when she arrived at school. She and Isobel had first met at college, many years ago. Isobel was so pretty and clever, and rather better dressed than the majority of girls. It had always surprised young Agnes Fogerty that they had become such firm friends. It had begun when the two discovered that they both came from the Cotswolds. Isobel's father was a bank manager at Stow-on-the-Wold, while Agnes's father was a shoemaker in Lulling.

Visits had been exchanged in the holidays, and Agnes had attended Isobel's splendid wedding. Marriage had taken her to Sussex where her husband owned several shops dealing in antique furniture.

The two girls kept in touch, although distance and Isobel's young children meant that they saw each other rarely. But whenever Isobel paid a visit to her parents at Stow she called to see Agnes, and the two picked up the threads of their friendship immediately.

When Isobel's husband died, Agnes had persuaded her to stay a few days at Thrush Green. Mrs White, her landlady, had a spare room then, and was glad to put it at the disposal of Agnes's old friend in her trouble.

Since then Agnes had spent several spells at Isobel's comfortable Sussex home. The children were now out in the world, and Isobel seemed glad of company. This letter, Miss Fogerty surmised, studying the envelope, might well contain another kind invitation to stay. In which case, it was a good thing that the new mackintosh 'awaited collection at her earliest convenience'. Isobel was always so beautifully dressed, and although she could never aspire to such elegance, at least she could look *respectable*.

She decided to enjoy reading the letter later and tucked the blue envelope into her handbag, and crossed the playground, nodding and smiling at the early arrivals who rushed to greet her. The asphalt, she noticed with her experienced teacher's eye, was quite dry again.

Thank heaven, the children would be able to play outside! She entered her splendid new classroom in good spirits.

Albert Piggott, on that Monday morning, was certainly not in good spirits. He had woken with a sharp pain in his chest and a severe headache.

He had no doubt about the cause of these symptoms. It was that dratted bath that his fool of a daughter had bullied him into—and he told her so.

'Don't talk soft, Dad,' Molly said tartly at breakfast, but secretly she felt a little guilty. Could he have caught a chill? In any case, it was absolutely necessary for him to be cleaned up, and she did not regret burning his disgusting garments.

'Well, wrap up when you go out,' said Molly. 'And I'll get you some cough mixture when I go down to Lulling.'

The old man continued to grumble throughout the day, and certainly by tea time, was flushed in the face and breathing heavily. Molly, trying to hide her alarm, persuaded him to go to bed early.

'He's not right,' she told Ben. 'I'm going to get the doctor to him if he's no better in the morning. Sometimes I wonder

if we oughtn't to settle here. He needs looking after, and there's
no one but me, now Nelly's gone. And another thing, we'll
have to be thinking of George's schooling soon. It's not fair
to send him here, there, and everywhere, for a week or so
at a time, as we move around. He won't learn nothing that
way.'

Ben nodded understandingly.

'I've been thinking too. I reckon we've got to face staying
put, and if you want that place to be Thrush Green, then that
suits me. But not in this house, love, and not until we can
get a place of our own.'

'But when will that be?' cried Molly, in despair. 'All we've
got is the fair, and would you ever want to give it up?'

'It looks as though I might have to,' said Ben slowly, and
began to tell her the problems and plans which had been
plaguing him for the last few months.

She listened in silence, and then put her hand on his.

'You did right to tell me. You shouldn't have kept all this
to yourself, Ben. We'll put our heads together and work out
what's best to be done, and find out more from Dick Hasler
too. You see, something'll turn up.'

A heavy thumping came from the bedroom above them.

'That's Dad,' said Molly. 'I promised him a cup of tea, and
clean forgot it.'

She crossed to the sink.

'You go and earn some honest pennies over the fair
there,' she smiled at Ben. 'We're going to need 'em in the
future.'

Some sixty miles away, Robert and Milly Bassett were

rejoicing in the doctor's verdict that a journey to Thrush Green could be undertaken at any time.

'But watch it!' he warned. 'Keep those tablets in your pocket, and don't ignore any warning signs. I have been in touch with your son-in-law, Doctor Lovell, and I know you will be well looked after.'

'And I intend to do the driving,' said Milly. 'Not on the motorway though. We'll take the old road, and stop at our old haunts on the way.'

'Good idea. But he's quite fit to drive, you know, as long as he stops if he feels the least bit tired.'

'I shall ring Joan tonight,' said Milly, when the doctor had gone. 'Won't it be lovely to see Thrush Green again?'

'I can't get there fast enough,' confessed Robert. 'Now that I know the business is safe in Frank's hands I have just given up worrying about it completely. It's wonderful to look forward to something. That's been half the trouble, I realize now, thinking about what one has done, or ought to have done, instead of looking ahead with hope. Thrush Green is going to set me up, and I'm not going to be such a fool as to jeopardise my health again. Life's too good to waste.'

'Come on Friday,' Joan said, when her mother telephoned. 'Everything's waiting, and everyone here wants to see you. Don't be surprised if all the flags are out!'

As it happened, Isobel's letter was not opened until after dinner time, for when Miss Fogerty entered her classroom she found that the fish tank had sprung a leak, and that the three gold-fish (named Freeman, Hardy and Willis by the adoring class), were gasping in a bare inch of water.

Miss Fogerty rushed for a bucket of water, and the net to catch the luckless fish, and spent a busy ten minutes on this errand of mercy and mopping up the floor and cupboard.

The children were entranced at the mess and added to the confusion by trying to help with their handkerchiefs, hastily-removed socks, and any other unsuitable piece of material which they could press into service. The amount of water which had come from one small tank was prodigious, and seemed to spread right across the room as well as flooding the cupboard below it. Naturally, it was the cupboard holding piles of new exercise books, the term's supply of coloured gummed squares, now living up to their name, tissue-paper, drawing paper, and thick paper used for painting. It was all most vexatious, and Miss Watson would not be pleased when she had to beg for more supplies, thought poor Agnes, wringing out the floorcloth.

She took her class across the playground, to the main building for morning prayers, and was obliged to postpone her account of the disaster until after assembly. Usually, she and Miss Watson had a minute or two together before Miss Fogerty seated herself at the ancient upright piano. Neither Miss Watson, nor any other member of the staff over the past ten years, seemed to have learned to play the piano, so that Miss Fogerty was obliged to face the music every morning.

Today Miss Watson was called to the telephone, and arrived a few minutes late. However, she faced the children with her usual calm smile, and prayers began.

Miss Fogerty noted that the hymn was not one of her favourites.

Raindrops are our diamonds
And the morning dew,
While for shining sapphires
We've the speedwell blue.

What was more, the thing was in four flats, a key which Miss Fogerty detested. However, she did her best, noticing yet again how sharp the older children's voices became towards the end of the hymn.

As the children were led away to their classrooms, Agnes told her headmistress of her misfortune.

'How tiresome,' said Miss Watson, 'and it would be dreadfully wasteful to have to throw away so much good material!

I think you had better spread out the sheets separately, Agnes dear, and dry them as best you can. We simply can't waste things.'

And easier said than done, thought Agnes rebelliously, as she crossed the playground. There were mighty few places to spread hundreds of sheets of wet paper in her classroom, and every time the door opened they would blow to the floor, and the children would rush to collect them, as well Miss Watson knew. There had been a chiding note too in her headmistress's voice, which annoyed her usually submissive assistant. Did she think that she had purposely damaged the fish tank? Good heavens, surely she wasn't being accused of wilful damage, or even of neglect? It was simply an act of God, well, perhaps not of God, thought Agnes hurriedly. He cared for all creatures after all, and must grieve for those poor fish who had been almost literally at their last gasp. No, it was a Complete Accident, she told herself firmly, and the only thing to do was to borrow another tank immediately for the poor things, and to endeavour to get her excited children into a calmer state of mind, ready for a good morning's work.

Consequently, it was not until cold mutton with jacket potatoes, followed by pink blancmange, had been dispatched that Miss Fogerty was at liberty to take out Isobel's letter in the peace of her empty classroom and read the news.

It gave her much food for thought, and distracted her attention for a while from her damp surroundings.

She was contemplating a move, Isobel wrote. Now that she was alone it seemed silly to keep up such a large house. The fuel bills alone were horrifying. The garden was far too big, and dear old Bates, who had come twice a week for more years than she cared to remember, had just told her that he must give up.

She would like to return to the Cotswolds, and proposed to look out for a small house, preferably in the Thrush Green area. Not that she was going to *rush* things. If possible, could kind Mrs White put her up for, say, a week while she got in touch with local estate agents? She would much prefer to stay there, in Agnes's company, than put up at the Fleece in Lulling. Hotel life was rather noisy at night, and the Fleece had no really quiet lounge during the day. Also it was a good distance from Agnes's house, and it was she that Isobel wanted to see, of course. But perhaps Agnes could find out if Mrs White would be agreeable?

Little Miss Fogerty shook her head sadly when she read that paragraph. Mrs White, she knew, would not be able to accommodate her old friend, for an ailing aunt now occupied the spare bedroom and looked like remaining there for some time to come.

The main news, of course, was wonderfully exciting. To think that Isobel might one day be her neighbour! It would be lovely to have her so close. She knew several people in Thrush Green and Lulling, and it was not very far from the Stow area where some of her relations still lived. How she hoped that Isobel would soon find somewhere suitable! She would help her with the move, of course. Perhaps next summer holidays?

Agnes's mind ran ahead happily, anticipating the joys to come. The only snag was this visit in the near future.

Where could she lodge? Mentally, Agnes reviewed the accommodation available near at hand. The Two Pheasants would never do. If Isobel thought the Fleece noisy, she would find the Two Pheasants insupportable, and there had been occasions when men had emerged *drunk* at closing time. Miss Watson, who lived so close to it, had told her so, and said how disagreeable it was.

She toyed with the idea of asking Miss Watson if she could put up her friend for a week. The two ladies had met, and enjoyed each other's company. But Agnes was not at all sure that Miss Watson deserved to have the honour of having Isobel as a paying guest, after her heartless handling of this morning's mishap.

Besides, Miss Watson had a brother who occasionally called unexpectedly, and the room might be needed for him.

And then little Miss Fogerty had a brainwave. She would call on the dear rector and see if he knew of likely lodgings. He and Dimity knew Isobel quite well, and had invited her to tea and bridge on several occasions. They would know the sort of place which would suit her. Somewhere in the parish there must be someone who would like to let a room to a charming, considerate lady like dear Isobel.

Out in the playground a whistle shrilled, and the children's roaring, whilst not actually stilled, was certainly diminished in volume.

Miss Fogerty put away her letter and her private problems, and went out to meet her class.

By mid-week, Albert Piggott was considerably worse, and was confined to his bed.

Doctor Lovell said that it would be wise for him to stay indoors for the rest of the week. His breathing was giving him pain, and he was seriously under weight, the legacy of a year or so's catering, or rather non-catering, for himself.

The wind had veered to the north-east, and Albert himself had forecast that it would stay in that quarter until Whitsun.

'You mark my words, gal,' he wheezed. 'We shan't have no more rain for a bit, but just this pesky dryin' wind to keep the buds from openin'. Won't get no bees venturing out in this cold weather.'

'Nor you, Dad,' said Molly, tucking in the bed clothes. 'You stay there, and I'll do my best to feed you up, like Doctor Lovell said.'

'It's no good,' she told Ben later. 'I'll have to stop here at least until the end of the week. You'll have to go on to Banbury alone. He's not fit to be left yet.'

Ben was philosophical about it. This had happened before, and was likely to happen again. It brought home to both of them the necessity to find a house and a job somewhere near the old man.

'One thing, our George isn't at school yet. Won't hurt him to stay here a few days. He's better off with you in the warm, than following me around in this wind.'

Albert Piggott was not a good patient. He never ceased to remind poor Molly that it was the unnecessary bathing which had reduced him to his present plight.

He toyed with the food which Molly so carefully prepared, pouring contumely upon such dainties as steamed fish and egg custard which he dismissed as 'dam' slops'. Molly had to stand over him to make sure that he took his medicine every four hours. He took to throwing off the bedclothes, complaining of heat, and occasionally hung out of the window in his flimsy pyjamas 'to get a breath of air'.

Molly was sometimes in despair. Only the threat of calling in the district nurse or, worse still, getting the old man into Lulling Cottage Hospital, kept her irascible patient in some sort of submission.

The fair was due to go on the Thursday. She spent the time washing and ironing Ben's clothes and packing the caravan with groceries and homemade pies and cakes.

'Lord!' commented Ben. 'How long am I supposed to be alone? I'll be back for you and George next Monday, I reckon. I'll never get through that lot in a month of Sundays.'

'You never know,' said Molly. 'You give me a ring Monday morning at the Two Pheasants. I've fixed it with Bob. Then we can see how things are.'

That afternoon she remembered, with shame, that she had not called to see the Youngs where she had worked so happily. She left her father asleep, took George by the hand, and walked across the green to the lovely old house.

The buds of May were being violently assaulted by the rough wind. Dry leaves of last autumn were flying pell-mell across the grass, and a great roaring came from the branches of the chestnut trees. Little eddies of dust whirled like miniature sand storms in the road, and the smoke from a bonfire in Harold Shoosmith's garden blew in a rapidly moving cloud towards the distant Lulling Woods.

It was a thoroughly unpleasant afternoon, and Molly was glad to gain the shelter of the walled garden. She made her way to the back door, and rang the bell. Joan opened it and enveloped her in a warm hug.

'Wonderful to see you. I meant to call, but heard Albert wasn't well, and thought you might be rather busy. Tell me the news.'

The two sat at the kitchen table where Joan had been ironing and gossiped happily. Molly looked with affection at her old place of work. Nothing much had changed, and she commented on it with pleasure.

Joan told her about her parents' visit. Molly, in turn, told her about their hopes to find a settled job one day.

'I'll keep my ears open,' Joan promised her. 'I know how clever Ben is with his hands. It shouldn't be difficult to find a job. The house business will be more difficult, I suspect, but I won't forget, and if I hear of anything I shall get in touch.'

Molly left a forwarding address before she went, and promised to look in before Ben claimed her again.

'No, I best not stay for a cup of tea, thank you,' she said, in answer to Joan's invitation. 'Dad's medicine's got to be got down him within half an hour, and that'll take some doing.'

She made her farewells, and set off again to face the biting wind. The children were streaming out of school, followed by Miss Fogerty.

To Molly's surprise, the little figure did not take a homeward path through the avenue, but struck across Thrush Green towards the rectory. Going to collect the parish magazine? Offering to help Miss Dimity with a bazaar or some such? Taking a message from Miss Watson about the hymns? Such surmises are part of the pleasures of country living.

But this time Molly had guessed wrongly, for Miss Fogerty's errand concerned dear Isobel, a lady whom Molly had never met.

Still wondering, she opened the door of Albert's cottage and went to collect the medicine.

8 More News of Lodgers

DOTTY HARMER's new lodger, Flossie, had settled in very well, and the fact that nothing had been heard from her last owner was a great relief to Dotty, who had grown much attached to the young spaniel.

The dog followed her everywhere, as if, having been abandoned once, she feared that it might happen again. Dotty was moved by this affection, and returned it tenfold. The two grew very close and the sight of Dotty, shadowed by the faithful golden cocker, became a familiar sight in Lulling and Thrush Green.

One windy afternoon the two descended the hill to Lulling High Street. Dotty carried a basket in each hand, with Flossie's lead intricately entangled with one of them. They made steady progress against the biting east wind, which reddened Dotty's nose and sent Flossie's ears streaming behind her.

Their destination was the Misses Lovelocks' house. Dotty was bearing a collection of contributions for the bazaar, and was glowing with the comfortable feeling of doing good.

'Why, Dotty dear, how kind!' cried Bertha, on opening the door. 'Do bring them in. We'll put them straight on the table. Everything's in the dining-room.'

That gloomy apartment was certainly transfigured. The mahogany table had been covered by an enormous white damask cloth, a relic of some Victorian linen cupboard, and upon it there jostled an odd collection of objects.

Dominating all were Ella's colourful contributions. Dimity had supplied a dozen or so dried flower-and-grass arrangements, which the Misses Lovelock wondered if they could sell, as everyone in the district was addicted to making such things, and the market might well be saturated. However, they had been accepted with cries of delight, and one could only wait and see.

More normal contributions, such as soap, handkerchiefs, pots of jam and other preserves were among the rest, and would obviously be snapped up, and Dotty began to put her contributions among them.

'Four pots of preserved boletus, the *edible* kind, naturally,' gabbled Dotty, placing four sinister looking jars on the table. Through the murky fluid, could be seen some toadstools of venomous appearance. Ada's jaw dropped, but she remained silent, with commendable control.

'And six pots of hedgerow jelly,' continued Dotty, diving into her basket. 'It's a mixture, you know, of sloes, black-berries, rosehips, elderberries and any other nourishing berries I could find. I thought "Hedgerow Jelly" on the label, would cover it nicely.'

'Yes, indeed,' said Ada faintly, noting the sediment at the bottom of the jars, and the hint of mildew on the top.

'Not much room to write all the ingredients on the label, you see,' said Dotty, standing back to admire the imposing array. 'But I'm sure people will understand.'

'I'm sure they will,' agreed Violet bravely. But whether they would actually *buy* a jar of something which looked certain to give the consumer 'Dotty's Collywobbles' – a disease known to all Dotty's friends – was another matter.

'You are so generous, Dotty dear,' quavered Bertha, averting her gaze from the jars. 'And now you must stay and have some tea. Ada has made some delicious scones with wholemeal flour which we ground ourselves in father's old pestle and mortar.'

'Exactly the sort of thing I love,' said Dotty. 'And Flossie too, if she may have a crumb or two?'

The old ladies made their way to the drawing-room for this modest repast and a great deal of genteel gossip in which a number of Lulling residents' characters would be shredded finely, in the most ladylike fashion.

That same afternoon, Dimity had crossed the road to her old home to broach a subject which she and Charles had discussed thoroughly since Miss Fogerty's visit.

Charles had been wholly in favour of suggesting that Isobel Fletcher should spend the proposed week's visit with Ella.

'They both get on very well,' he said. 'Much the same age. And then Thrush Green is so central for the little trips she may wish to make for viewing places. I'm sure she would be perfectly happy.'

Dimity had some private doubts.

Everyone liked Isobel. She was kind, charming, and elegant. Ella had always spoken warmly of her, and admired her quick brain.

But Isobel was used to comfort. Her husband had been a prosperous man, and his wife was provided with a beautiful home and everything she could possibly desire. Could she stand the rough-and-ready hospitality which Ella would provide? And what about that all-pervading tobacco smoke? And the lack of punctuality in producing meals?

The meals themselves gave Dimity no fears. Ella had a surprisingly good way with food, and was meticulous about its preparation. The house might be a little dusty and untidy, but Ella's cooking arrangements could not be faulted. The snag was that she might well decide to make a chicken terrine at eleven in the morning, and hope to have it cold, with salad, at one oclock. Ella never seemed to have mastered the time factor in all her activities.

However, she was now on her way to put the proposition to her old friend. She found her sitting by the window doing the crossword puzzle.

'Funny minds these chaps must have,' said Ella, putting aside the paper. 'This clue "Makes waterproof" is "*Caulks*", and the next one is "Sea travel" which is "*Cruise*", so that makes "Corkscrews", d'you see?'

'No, I don't, dear, but I've something to tell you, and I must get back to take the cat's supper out of the oven, so I musn't linger.'

'And what is that spoilt animal having this evening?'

'Just a little rabbit. Nothing very special.'

'Lucky old cat! Well, come on, what's bothering you?'

Dimity launched into the account of Isobel Fletcher's need of lodgings for a week while she consulted agents about the possibility of buying a house in the neighbourhood. She explained Miss Fogerty's dilemma. Mrs White would not be able to put her up, as she had done. She *could*, of course, stay at the Fleece, but if Ella were willing . . .? The question hung in mid-air among the blue smoke from Ella's cigarette.

'Of course I'm willing,' replied Ella. 'I'm very fond of Isobel, and should be delighted to have her here. The only thing is, would she be comfortable?'

Trust dear Ella to come directly to the point, thought Dimity, with some relief.

'I'm sure she will be,' said Dimity bravely. 'If you like, I'll come over and help you make up the spare bed, and empty the cupboards, and so on.'

And give an expert eye to Isobel's comfort, she thought privately.

'When will it be? Any idea?'

'None, I'm afraid, but fairly soon, I imagine. Shall I let Agnes Fogerty know, or will you? I know she wants to write very soon.'

'I'll catch her after school,' said Ella. 'One thing though, I'm not letting Isobel pay me. It'll be a pleasure to have her here.'

'Well, you must sort that out between you,' said Dimity rising to go. 'It will be so nice to see her again, and I do so hope she finds somewhere to live nearby.'

'Unless she gets snapped up by somebody in Sussex before that,' said Ella shrewdly. 'She's eminently marriageable, from all viewpoints.'

'Oh, I don't think that will happen,' replied Dimity, slightly shocked. 'She's still grieving for her husband, you know. They were quite devoted.'

She opened the door to see a few children straggling across the green from the village school.

'Out already?' cried Ella. 'Here, I'll cut across now and see Agnes. No time like the present, and she can catch the afternoon post, if she looks slippy!'

Ben Curdle had departed on his way to Banbury, and Molly was left to cope with George and Albert as best she could.

The old man's temper did not improve. The doctor forbade his going outside in the bitter wind, which still prevailed, and Albert worried about the church and the way in which it was being looked after.

The rector had asked one of the Cooke boys to take on Albert's duties temporarily. The Cooke family was numerous and rather slap-dash, but there was no one else free to lend a hand and Jimmy Cooke had agreed to 'keep an eye on things'.

'And that's about all he will do,' growled Albert. 'And I won't be surprised to find me tools missing. Light-fingered lot them Cookes. Always on the look-out for somethin' to pinch.'

Molly tried to turn a deaf ear to the old man's constant complaining. How right Ben was to insist that they did not live with her father! Whatever the future held, that was certain. Look after him she would, as best she could, but to see dear Ben and young George suffering the gloomy and insulting behaviour of the miserable old fellow, was more than she could bear.

'If that's what old age brings you to,' thought Molly, attacking some ironing, 'I hopes as I dies young!'

Not that all old people were as trying as her father, she had to admit. Dear old Dr Bailey, for instance, had always been a happy man, even in his last long illness, and Mr Bassett, who would be arriving for his holiday that very afternoon, always had a cheerful word for everyone.

Perhaps education helped? Molly pondered on this as she ironed a pillowslip. If your mind was full of knowledge, then perhaps you did not worry overmuch about your body and its ills? It brought her again to the question of George's future. A sound schooling he was going to have, come what may, and he could not do better than start at Thrush Green School with Miss Watson and Miss Fogerty. He was going to have a better start in life than his father. Poor Ben, she remembered, had been unable to read and write, with any competence, when

they first met, and she herself had acted as teacher. She had
certainly had a willing—even amorous—pupil, and within a
month or so he had mastered his difficulties. But he had never
forgotten the humiliation of having to confess his ignorance
for so many years, and he was as determined as Molly that
George should never suffer in the same way.

Well, the next step was to look out for a suitable job for
Ben. Once the Bassetts were settled in, she would have
another talk with Joan Young, and perhaps walk down to that
new Job Centre in Lulling to see if there were any openings
for a hard-working man like her dear Ben.

Whoever employed him, thought Molly loyally, would be
lucky. There was no one—simply no one—like her Ben.

There was a splendid sunset as Molly finished her ironing.
Bands of gold, scarlet and violet clouds transfigured the
western sky, and the dark mass of Lulling Woods was
silhouetted against the blaze of glory.

The rooks were flapping homeward, their black satin
feathers catching the light. Albert Piggott's cat sat on the sun-
warmed wall of the Two Pheasants and enjoyed the last of the
daylight.

Betty Bell, who was cleaning Miss Fogerty's schoolroom,
stopped her ministrations to admire the spectacle. Just like a
jumper she'd knitted once! All different bands of colour, she
remembered, and no end of trouble with the vee neck. But
what a gorgeous sight!

Miss Harmer would have a good view from her cottage,
and Mr Shoosmith, next door to the school, would see that
sunset even better from the bedroom she had done out that

morning. Did you a power of good to see something pretty like that, thought Betty, returning to her desk polishing, much refreshed.

A car drew up outside the Youngs' gate, and before the doors were opened, Joan ran out to set the gates open.

Slowly the car drew into the drive. Out stepped Milly Bassett, to be enveloped in her daughter's embrace, and then, rather more slowly, Robert emerged.

He looked pale and rather shaky, but he stood erect and took in great breaths of fragrant air. His face was alight with pleasure.

'Just what I've been longing for,' he told Joan, holding out his arms. 'To come home again!'

Part Two

Change at Thrush Green

9 Visitors to Thrush Green

THERE now began for Robert Bassett a period of intense joy.

It was as if all his senses had been sharpened by the shock of his recent illness. He saw, with fresh awareness, the small beauties around him, and marvelled that he had not enjoyed them before.

The lilac was beginning to break in the garden, each fragrant plume composed of hundreds of exquisite flowerets. Grape hyacinths spread a carpet of vivid blue beneath the burgundy-red stems of the dogwood bushes.

He came across a thrush's nest, cleverly hidden in the crutch of the hawthorn hedge, and admired the smooth mud lining, as beautifully rounded as the speckled breast of the bird that sat so patiently upon the four turquoise blue eggs.

Everything delighted him. He ventured from the garden to Thrush Green, observing the pattern of blue smoke from cottage chimneys which matched the distant blur of Lulling Woods. He sat on the seat near the statue of Nathaniel Patten and gloried in the warmth of the sun upon his face, the droplets spangling a spider's web, the timid advances of Albert Piggott's cat whose curiosity had overcome her fear, and the rough comfort of the blackthorn walking stick in his hand.

How right W. H. Davies had been, thought Robert, when
he wrote:

> What is this life
> If full of care
> We have no time
> To stand and stare?

This was the first time, in a long life, that he had savoured
to the full the pleasures of his senses. He remembered the
extraordinary sensations he had felt, when bedbound, on his
sudden awareness of the inanimate objects in the bedroom.
That had been the beginning of his new response to his
surroundings, although weakness then had blurred some of the
pleasure.

Now, with ever-growing strength, he gave thanks for the
miracles around him, and his ability to recognise them.

Sickness, reflected Robert, changed a man. He thought of
the invalids he had known. How often he had dismissed their
querulousness and complaints as the outcome of self-pity!
He knew better now.

It was not only with themselves and their pain that the sick
were concerned. They worried for others. They grieved for
the work they were causing, for the disruption of other people's
lives, the sapping of their energy, the tensions within a family,
and the awful possibility of increasing helplessness.

He had been lucky, he thought soberly. Lucky to have had
his darling Milly as constant support, a doctor he trusted, and
a loving family. Lucky too, to have realised this further truth,
that the sick are sad, not only for themselves, but for those
they love. He would never forget it.

And luckiest of all, thought Robert, gazing around him, to be at peace in Thrush Green on a bright May morning.

Albert Piggott had thrived under Molly's care, and Doctor Lovell assured the girl that her father could cope perfectly well without her presence.

'I'll keep an eye on him,' he promised her. 'I gather from Bob Jones that you've arranged for a midday meal for him at the Two Pheasants. He should do well now that the weather's warmer.'

Molly told him of her fears that he would need more care as the years passed, and of their plans to settle within easy distance of the old man.

'Well, it happens to us all,' agreed the doctor. 'But don't completely upset your lives for Albert. He's by way of being a bit of a fraud, you know.'

He laughed to soften his words, and Molly smiled too.

'Oh, we knows him well enough, Doctor! But it don't alter the fact that he's gettin' an old man. I wish his Nelly hadn't left him. She took good care of him.'

'They weren't exactly turtle-doves,' commented the doctor. 'It was plain that it couldn't last.'

'I know she was a right trollop in her ways,' agreed Molly earnestly, 'but she kept that house spotless, and her cooking was just beautiful. Dad was lucky to get her. After all, you can't expect *everything* in marriage.'

Doctor Lovell tried to hide his amusement as he drove off on his rounds. There was something very refreshing about Molly's attitude to the wedded state. Obviously, good housewifery was rated rather more highly than fidelity in Molly's scale of reckoning. Her own marriage, he knew, was an outstanding success. So, he thought, was his own to Ruth. They were both lucky to have found the right partners. It did not look as if Albert would find another to give him companionship in his old age.

Ah well! What could he expect? He was a thoroughly selfish old man, and he only hoped that Molly would not put her marriage in jeopardy by trying to live with Albert Piggott.

Not that it was likely, thought Doctor Lovell, turning his car into the village of Nidden. Ben would see to that.

The early days of May followed each other with increasing warmth and fragrance. Spring-cleaning was finished in a spurt of energy. Blankets blew upon clothes-lines, carpets were beaten, curtains and bedspreads washed, and good housewives congratulated themselves upon the amount of work which could be accomplished, given bright sunshine and fair winds.

Dimity had kept her word and helped Ella to prepare for Isobel's arrival. The spare-room awaited her, with cupboards and drawers emptied and relined with clean paper, furniture glossy with polish, and a vase of pheasant-eye narcissi on the bedside table.

'D'you think she'll be comfortable?' asked Ella, unusually anxious.

'Of course,' replied Dimity reassuringly.

'I'm not sure just when she'll arrive,' went on Ella, 'so I thought I'd whip up an omelette for this evening. There's plenty of salad. I wonder if that will be enough?'

'Isobel was always a small eater,' said Dimity. 'And no doubt you've plenty of fruit, and cheese.'

'Dotty brought me some goat's cheese this morning,' said Ella, 'but I'm not putting *that* on the cheese board. Don't want the poor girl struck down with Dotty's Collywobbles while she's here.'

'No, indeed,' agreed Dimity. 'Now, I must get back to Charles. He has a diocesan meeting at six, miles away, and I want to make sure that he has a good tea.'

She hurried across the road to the bleak rectory, leaving Ella to survey her preparations with a critical eye.

'Ah well,' she said at last. 'Can't do any more now. Time I had a cigarette before dear old Isobel arrives.'

She settled down on the window seat, and began to roll a pungent cigarette. But before she had a chance to light it, a small pale-blue glossy car stopped at the gate, and Isobel emerged.

Throwing the cigarette into the battered tobacco tin, Ella hurried to open the gate, enfolding Isobel in a great bear-hug on the way.

'Wonderful to see you,' she boomed. 'Had a good trip? My word, this looks a handsome vehicle!'

She surveyed the car with much admiration.

'It's an Alfa Romeo,' said Isobel, 'and it certainly got me here in record time today. Traffic was amazingly light, and I know my way so well, of course, there was no need to stop for map-reading or asking people.'

'All "strangers in these parts" anyway, I find,' said Ella, helping with Isobel's case which was as sleek and elegant as the car. 'I'm going to put on the kettle. It can boil while I show you your room. That is, if you'd like a cup of tea?'

'More than anything in the world,' said Isobel, following her hostess.

The arrival of the beautiful Alfa Romeo had been noted by Harold Shoosmith who was walking across the green to call upon Charles Henstock.

Harold loved cars, and was beginning to think that it was high time that he parted with the ancient Daimler which had served him so well for years. But what to buy in its place?

All through his life he had bought cars made in Britain. In the long years abroad, his succession of British cars had been a precious link with home, and a source of admiration to friends overseas. Now he found himself looking in vain for the sort of small, distinguished and well-finished vehicle which he wanted.

Parking in Lulling High Street was no easy task with the gallant old Daimler. Its petrol consumption grew as the years passed. The time had come, Harold knew, with sadness, when he must part with it. There were several foreign cars on the market which attracted him, but loyalty to British makers made him hesitant to look at overseas models.

But Isobel's pale blue beauty was certainly an eye-catcher. He looked it over, from a distance, as he waited for someone to come to the rectory door.

Charles greeted him and took him into his study.

'Dimity's gone to take some magazines to Dotty Harmer,' he told his friend. 'Do sit down.'

'I won't keep you long,' replied Harold. He was thinking how dark and cold this room always seemed. Today, with the warm May sunshine flooding the world with golden light, it seemed incredible that this bleak study remained untouched by its ambience.

'I came for the sweep's address,' said Harold. 'Betty Bell tells me that we should have had the chimneys done a month ago. She can't remember the new chap's name, and neither can I, of course.'

'Surely, you have Potter from Lulling?'

'He died last year, I'm told.'

The rector looked shocked.

'I'm truly grieved to hear that. He was not one of my parishioners, of course, but I should like to have called on him during his last illness.'

'He didn't really have one, according to Betty,' answered Harold. 'Dropped down on someone's hearth with the flue brush still in his hand, so she says. "A lovely way to go," was her comment, "but made a terrible mess of the carpet." I'm sorry to have brought bad news.'

'Not at all. Not at all,' replied the rector, pulling himself together. 'But about this new man. I'm sure we are as nonplussed as you are, as we always had poor Potter. Have you any clues?'

'Betty tells me that he lives at the other side of Lulling Woods. He clears cesspits and farm drains, does a bit of poaching, has had three wives and rears ferrets.'

'John Boston, without a doubt,' said the rector immediately. 'Rather a rough diamond, but a very useful member of the community, when he's not in prison. I have a soft spot for John, I must admit. I'm sure he'll do your chimneys beautifully.'

He reached for a piece of paper, and wrote down the address.

'It might be best to call on him, Harold. I doubt if he can read very well.'

He handed over the slip of paper.

'Many thanks, Charles. I'll do that. Now, tell me, whose is that dazzling little car outside Ella's?'

'It must belong to Isobel Fletcher,' responded the rector. 'I know she was expected today, but I imagined she would arrive later than this. A charming woman. Have you met her?'

'No, I'm afraid not.'

'Then you must,' said the rector firmly, accompanying his visitor into the sunshine of Thrush Green. 'She's here for a week, I know, and may settle here permanently if she finds a suitable house.'

He looked about him with some surprise.

'Why, it's quite warm out here! I think I shall leave my paperwork and do a little gardening instead.'

'A very sound idea,' agreed his friend.

Albert Piggott, partially restored to health, was doing a little light gardening himself in the churchyard, Harold noticed, as he returned to his own home.

These days, the churchyard was very much easier to maintain than it had been when Harold first came to Thrush Green some years earlier.

It had been his idea to clear the whole area, to put the gravestones round the low wall which surrounded the plot, and to level the ground so that a motor mower could be used.

There had been some opposition to this scheme, but there was considerable pride in the improved tidiness of Albert's domain, and certainly the little church of St Andrew's was more attractive now in its very spacious setting.

Albert Piggott was the last person to admit that his labours had been rendered considerably lighter by the new layout. From the first, he had refused to touch the motor mower, and the Cooke boy, who had been acting as locum during Albert's illness, had taken on the mowing from the start, and proved remarkably reliable.

Albert's job consisted of a certain amount of hoeing and weeding, the upkeep of the gravel path round the church, and the pruning of the shrubs.

On this particular afternoon he was plucking groundsel from the gravel. It was about the easiest job he could find outside in the sunshine. Also he was in full view of the rectory, should the rector wish to see him at work, and very handy for the Two Pheasants.

He had demolished a helping of steak and kidney pie, with mashed potatoes and tinned peas, at that hostelry, some two hours earlier, paid for by Ben and Molly in advance.

'Not a patch on Nelly's cooking,' he had grumbled to the landlord, who affected deafness. If he took note of all Albert's whinings, he told himself, he'd be in the local loony bin in next to no time. Best to ignore the old misery!

Now, with bending, Albert was suffering from indigestion, and feeling more than usually sorry for himself. Visions of Nelly's pies and roast joints floated before his eyes. No doubt about it, you never got a ha'p'orth of heartburn after Nelly's cooking!

He collected a few more handfuls of groundsel, threw

them on to the compost heap, hidden in a remote corner of the churchyard, and wandered across the road to his cottage.

He rummaged in a jamjar which served as his medicine chest, discovered an indigestion tablet, and sat sucking it morosely as he surveyed the kitchen.

Nothing had been done to it since Molly left, apart from a little desultory washing of crockery and cutlery. The stove was dingy. The floor was dirty. The windows were misty with grime, and dust lay everywhere. It needed a woman's hand, thought Albert sentimentally. Here he was, an invalid, with no one to look after him, deserted by his wife and daughter, left to fend for himself in his old age. It was enough to bring tears to your eyes, that it was!

His thoughts turned again to Nelly. She wasn't everybody's choice, of course. For one thing, she must have turned the scales at sixteen stone, and she had a laugh that fairly made your head throb. Then she was a stickler for cutting down on the drink—a bad thing for a man who enjoyed the occasional glass. She was a nagger too, when the spirit moved her. No, she had been lucky to have found someone like himself to put up with her ways, decided Albert.

But there—she was a real stunner of a cook, and could be very loving when she wanted anything. Money, for instance. She wasn't above taking a pound note out of his wallet on the sly, if he didn't pass it over when requested.

And then that flirting with the oil man! That was enough to turn anyone's stomach, remembered Albert. And finally, to leave a good husband and home to live with the fellow! It was unforgivable.

Albert's indigestion grew worse at the very thought of Nelly's infidelity. What if she was a wonderful cook, and a superb housewife? Her morals were no better than an alley cat's. Come to think of it, an alley cat probably behaved more circumspectly than his wife, he decided, rubbing the pain in his diaphragm.

He was better off without her, dirt, indigestion and all. He stumbled across to the sink, and filled the kettle. A cup of tea might settle his tempestuous inside. Nothing like a cup of tea for comfort!

Sniffing slightly with self-pity, Albert fumbled among the dirty dishes on the draining-board and found himself a relatively clean cup.

*   *   *

The golden May day ended in a blazing sunset. The rooks flew home to Lulling Woods, and children pleaded to stay up to play.

The bronze statue of Nathaniel Patten on Thrush Green caught the last of the light, glinting like gold. Lilac, narcissi and early stocks breathed out a heady fragrance, and all was at peace.

Two miles away, a train drew out of Lulling Station. Only one passenger had alighted, and the ticket collector tried to hide his amazement as he took the ticket in his hand. .

No words were exchanged, but he watched the traveller out of sight with the greatest excitement.

Purposefully, the large figure waddled towards the town. In one hand it carried a case. In the other, a handbag and a bag of groceries.

For better or for worse, Nelly Piggott was returning to Thrush Green.

10 Ella's Party

FOR little Miss Fogerty, the arrival of her friend Isobel spelt happy excitement.

Modest and retiring by nature, the very fact that she was immured in the classroom all day, and that her lodgings were a little way from the centre of Thrush Green, meant that she had made few friends in the neighbourhood.

Be civil to all,
But familiar with few,

was a precept hung upon the shop wall of her father, the shoemaker. It certainly summed up his attitude to his customers and to his chapel acquaintances. There was little entertaining done. It was not only that money was short. It was an inherent timidity which restrained the shoemaker from giving cause for comment or ridicule. He was a great one for 'keeping himself to himself', and Agnes took after him.

The inhabitants of Thrush Green were fond of her. Many of them remembered her from their schooldays, and always with affection and respect. But Agnes Fogerty was not the sort of person in whom one could confide – or, for that matter, in whom one could arouse laughter or rage. Always kind, always ladylike, shiningly honest and conscientious, these very attributes seemed to surround her with an invisible guard which no one had completely penetrated.

Except Isobel. Perhaps it was because they had first met when they were both young and vulnerable, thrown together in the alien world of college, and grateful for the common memories of their Cotswold background. This friendship had survived the years, the changes of fortune and the many miles between them.

To Isobel it was a source of comfort and quiet pleasure. To Agnes it was much more. She never ceased to wonder that Isobel, so much cleverer, so much more beautiful, so much more prosperous, could still enjoy her own, limited company. Their friendship was an inspiration to the quiet school teacher, and did much to mitigate the fact that she had so few friends at Thrush Green.

Of course, she counted her headmistress, Miss Watson, as a friend, and was glad to hear her confidences and hopes. In times of stress, Agnes knew that she had been of real help, and the thought warmed her. But that inherent timidity, inculcated by her father, made her careful of overstepping the bounds of propriety.

Miss Watson was *The Head*. She was *An Assistant*. Nothing could alter those two facts, and Agnes was careful to keep a certain distance between them, as was only right and proper. Although, sometimes, she had a pang of regret.

It seemed so silly that two grown women, both single, both lonely at times, should not become closer in friendship. And yet, any overtures must, of course, come from Miss Watson. It would look *pushing* if she herself made the running.

Miss Fogerty remembered how much she had enjoyed

being of use to Miss Watson on one or two occasions when accident or ill-health had indisposed her headmistress. She was always so grateful for any little kindnesses done, thought Agnes, and for this generosity of spirit it was worth ignoring the minor pinpricks which daily companionship sometimes brought, such as the wounding words on the recent occasion of the leaking fish tank. Perhaps she was over-sensitive about these things? Or perhaps she was getting prickly in her old age?

Well, whatever the cause, the fact that Isobel was in Thrush Green for a week, wiped out any unhappy feelings. For the next few days she intended to see her old friend as often as her duties would allow.

The May sunshine which warmed Thrush Green only increased the inner glow of little Miss Fogerty's heart. An invitation to drinks from Ella was 'accepted with the greatest pleasure' and, in this case, with perfect truth.

Robert Bassett's returning strength was noted with much relief at Thrush Green. Already he had spent an evening playing bridge at Winnie Bailey's in the company of his wife, the Hursts who lived next door at Tullivers, and Charles and Dimity Henstock.

His daily walk grew a little longer, and he began to plan a walk downhill to Lulling in the near future.

Joan and Ruth and his son-in-law Doctor Lovell were beginning to congratulate themselves upon the patient's well-being when something happened to jog them out of their complacency.

Robert had gone out on his own along the quiet lane to Nod and Nidden. Milly was going to catch him up, but a phone call delayed her, and it was some ten minutes later that she left the house.

To her horror, she discovered her husband flat on his face, his head upon the grass verge, and his legs in the road. His breathing was laboured, his lips blue, and his hands were cold.

She whipped off her jacket and flung it over the prostrate form, and luckily, at that moment, Willie Bond the postman, came along on his bicycle.

'Lor!' was his comment. 'Has he croaked?'

'Of course not!' retorted Milly, with understandable asperity. 'Could you run to the Youngs' and get help, Willie?'

'Ah! That I will,' responded Willie, throwing a fat leg over the saddle with maddening slowness.

He pedalled off, and Milly felt in her husband's waistcoat pocket for the magic tablets which Doctor Lovell had pre-scribed. She could not find them, and had to content herself with chafing the cold hands, and putting a scarf under her husband's head.

A minute later, Joan arrived, flushed with anxiety.

'John's on his way with the car,' she said. 'Luckily, he was still in the surgery.'

Robert's eyelids began to flicker, and he attempted to lift his head.

'I'm all right,' he murmured. 'I'm all right. I'm all right. I'm all right.'

But the two anxious women knew that he was not, and saw with relief that Doctor Lovell's car was approaching.

Within twenty minutes Robert Bassett was back in bed, and the hopes of all had plummeted.

*   *   *

The inhabitants of Thrush Green were united in their sadness when the news broke. But prognostications of what might happen differed, of course.

Betty Bell told Harold Shoosmith that her uncle went just the same way. First time, recovered. Second, snuffed out!

Albert Piggott was of the opinion that a new heart put in might be the answer. Why, that chap in South Africa – Christine Someone, wasn't it? – had put a whole hatful of hearts in dozens of poor souls like Mr Bassett. To his mind, it was worth trying. He only wished this Doctor Christine did lungs as well. Pity he lived such a long way off.

Dotty Harmer told Dimity Henstock that she feared that Robert Bassett had eaten far too much animal fat during his life, and this was the consequence.

'I tried, time and time again, to wean him on to a vegetable diet, but with no success,' sighed Dotty. 'Men are very obstinate.'

Naturally, it was a subject of general interest at Ella's small party.

Miss Fogerty had dressed with care. As chief visitor's friend she felt that she owed it to Isobel to appear in her best. She wore a brown silk frock with a small ivory-coloured lace modesty vest let into the front, and her mother's cornelian brooch. She had spent some time trying to decide if her seed pearls could be worn as well, but a horror of being overdressed decided her against them. The brooch was quite enough.

As the weather was so dry and warm it was unnecessary to wear a coat, but Miss Fogerty folded an Indian shawl and put it prudently in her brown leather handbag. It might be chilly later.

She set out from her lodgings in innocent excitement. Outings were rare occasions, and to be the acknowledged close friend of dear Isobel, among her Thrush Green neighbours, meant a great deal to Agnes.

The Henstocks, Winnie Bailey and the Hursts were already there when she knocked timidly at Ella's front door. Isobel came forward to kiss her, and the assembled company greeted her warmly.

'Now, what's it to be?' enquired Ella. She was dispensing drinks with her usual forthright confidence. Some women would have delegated the job to one of the men, but not Ella.

'Tio Pepe? Or a sweet sherry? Gin and lime? Gin and tonic? Dubonnet? Or I've tomato juice and pineapple juice if you like the soft stuff.'

'The dry sherry, please,' said Miss Fogerty. Her dear father had approved of a little dry sherry, she remembered, and despised those who preferred a fruitier variety. Not that sherry had played much part in the shoemaker's house. At Christmas time there might be a bottle of sherry in the cupboard, but it was certainly looked upon as a luxury.

'Can't think what's happened to Dotty,' said Ella. 'Anyone seen her?'

'She was picking greenstuff for the rabbits,' said Winnie. 'I noticed her when I called to see if I could do anything for the Bassetts.'

'Hope she hasn't forgotten,' said Ella. 'And how was poor old Robert?'

'In bed, resting. I didn't go up. He seems to be sleeping quite a bit.'

'It's too bad, after the marvellous progress he was making,' said Dimity. 'I do hope he won't try to get back to that business of his. Time he retired.'

'I agree,' said Charles. 'I take it that the Youngs won't be coming here this evening?'

'No, they cried off,' said Ella.

'Coo-ee!' called a voice.

'Dotty!' exclaimed Ella, hurrying to the door.

They heard voices and footsteps, and in came Dotty, accompanied by Harold Shoosmith.

'We thought you might have forgotten,' said Dimity.

'Good heavens, no!' replied Dotty. 'Why, I went up to change a full hour ago.'

'My fault entirely,' broke in Harold. 'I waylaid her, and took her to see my tulips. Just showing off really.'

'Well, come and meet Isobel Fletcher,' said Ella, leading him across to the room.

Harold found himself standing in front of an extremely pretty woman. There was a gentle serenity and poise about her which immediately appealed to him.

'How do you do?' said Isobel holding out her hand, and as Harold held it, he was suddenly reminded of something which he had read recently. Ellen Terry, if he remembered aright, had talked of 'a holy palmer's kiss, a sympathy of the skin', when some hands met in a clasp. For the first time, he was conscious of it, and was strangely stirred.

They talked of Thrush Green, and of her efforts to find a home nearby.

'I used Williams and Frobisher,' Harold told her, 'when I was seeking a house here. I'd tried four or five other estate agents, but they would keep sending me details of derelict oast-houses and windmills, or manor houses with twenty-two bedrooms and no bath, until I was nearly driven insane. I must say Williams and Frobisher were much more practical.'

'I'll try them tomorrow,' promised Isobel. 'And now I see Ella beckoning to me, so you must excuse me.'

She made her way towards her hostess, and Charles Henstock took her place at Harold's side. If his old friend appeared slightly bemused, the good rector was not conscious of it.

'An excellent party. Ella is so good at this sort of thing, and I always enjoy coming to this house. Something very snug about a low ceiling. The rectory could do with the ceilings lowered by a yard or so. But how would one begin?'

'That's beyond me,' confessed Harold. 'Tell me, how long is Miss Fletcher staying?'

'*Mrs* Fletcher, Harold.'

'Oh, I'm afraid I didn't catch that when we were introduced.'

'I never catch *anyone's* name,' admitted the rector. 'It is a great disability, particularly if one is a parson.'

Harold was looking thoughtful.

'Are you feeling all right?' asked the rector. 'Not finding the room too warm?'

'No, no!' said Harold. 'I'm quite well. An excellent party, as you say. Is Mrs Fletcher's husband here somewhere?'

The rector's chubby face grew sad.

'I am sorry to say that he died last year. A great blow for dear Isobel. They were a devoted couple. It's one of the reasons for the move, I gather. Her present house is really too big now.'

Despite the melancholy news of Isobel's husband's demise, Harold's spirits appeared to revive at once.

'More sherry?' asked Ella, swimming into their ken.

'Thank you, thank you,' said Harold heartily, proffering his glass.

Across the green, as dusk fell, and the lights began to shine from cottage windows, Joan Young and her husband were looking ahead.

Upstairs, Robert Bassett slept fitfully, with Milly sitting in an armchair beside him. Her hands were busy with knitting, her mind busy with plans for the future.

John Lovell, her doctor son-in-law, knew her good sense and had answered her questions honestly. It would be best to face retirement now, to wind up the business, and to find an easily run place near the family at Thrush Green, he had said.

'Would you want to come back to this house?' he asked. 'It's lovely, I know, and it's Robert's, but you'd need resident help, wouldn't you? Have you and Robert ever discussed it?'

'Only very lightly,' admitted Milly. 'We've always had the idea of coming back here to end our days—'

Her mouth quivered suddenly, and she looked down quickly.

John patted her shoulder.

'Don't upset yourself. He's got a good few years yet, you know, if he takes care. We'll work out something together.'

Downstairs, Edward was putting forward a suggestion or two.

'I've been thinking about this for some time. Ever since we had a good look at the stables the other day. They would convert into a beautiful little house of one or two floors, ideal for the parents.'

'But this house is theirs!' protested Joan. 'We're the ones who should move out!'

'I agree absolutely,' said Edward, 'but it would have to be altered. The ground floor would make a splendid flat for them, and we could move up to the first floor and open up the attics for bedrooms, if that would suit everyone better than the stable plan.'

'Would it cost the earth?'

'Well, the architect's fees won't need to be found,' said Edward, smiling, 'and I'm sure we could get a loan for this work. After all, we're thinking of providing homes for two families, aren't we?'

Joan looked at him with affection.

'You've been thinking about this for a long time, haven't you?'

'For years,' confessed Edward. 'I've been longing to convert the stables for some time now, and this seems to be the moment to have a go.'

'We can't do anything until Father's over this attack,' said Joan. 'But we'll have a word with Mother in a day or two, just to prepare the ground. I must say, I should be much happier if they were under our eye. They've been so good to us always.'

'Well, it's their choice, of course. All this is theirs, and, if need be, we must go house-hunting ourselves.'

'Somehow,' said Joan, 'I don't think it will come to that.'

Agnes Fogerty had been invited to supper after the guests had gone, and very enjoyable she had found this meal.

Afterwards, the three women washed up and between them achieved a degree of unusual tidiness in Ella's kitchen.

That done, Isobel accompanied Miss Fogerty along the road to her home. The air was soft and balmy, auguring well for another beautiful spring day on the morrow.

'No, I won't come in,' Isobel replied in answer to Agnes's invitation. 'I know you've things to get ready for school tomorrow, and I must get back to Ella's.'

They parted affectionately at Agnes's gate, and Isobel retraced her steps.

How snug it all looked at Thrush Green, she thought! The houses sat as comfortably as cats before a fire. If only she were lucky enough to find one before long!

Well, tomorrow she would go to see Williams and Frobisher, as recommended by that nice sensible man who lived across the green.

She looked at his house now, a secure bulk dimly visible against the night sky. In a downstairs window, a reading lamp was alight. It looked as though he might be happily settled in there.

She only hoped that she might be as lucky with Williams and Frobisher as he had been, Isobel thought, as she opened Ella's gate.

11 Village Gossip

AS Nelly Piggott (*née* Tilling) plodded along Lulling High Street from the station, she looked ahead, with some trepidation, to the kind of welcome she might expect from her husband, Albert.

She had parted from him after a fierce quarrel, but this was only the culmination of weeks of disgust with Albert. He was mean, he was dirty, he was bad-tempered. He drank, he grumbled, he swore. Why she had ever married him, Nelly wondered, shifting her case to the other hand, heaven alone knew.

Well, to be honest, she admitted to herself, she did know. She needed a home. Her own cottage had been sold by the owner, and she had turned down those on offer at the time. Ted and Bessie Allen at the Drovers' Arms at Lulling Woods, had put her up for a few weeks, and she had enjoyed scrubbing out the bar for them.

But a woman needs a place of her own, and Lulling Woods was too quiet for Nelly's taste. Thrush Green seemed just the right setting for a woman of Nelly's sociable habits. The fact that the village school needed a cleaner, just at that time, was another advantage.

And then there was Albert Piggott. Or rather, Albert Piggott's cottage. It was handy for the school, and the bus to

Lulling, and looked out on the green where there was always
something going on.

Moreover, the cottage was filthy, and Nelly longed to get
at it with plenty of hot water, soap and a stout scrubbingbrush. It was a challenge. Dirt was always a challenge to
Nelly, and she responded to this one with energy and courage.
Within a week the place was transformed, and looking back
upon those early days Nelly realised she had been happy, not
because of Albert, but because of the satisfaction of cleaning
his house.

Not that he was unappreciative. He was particularly grateful
for the magnificent meals she cooked, and the fact that she was
obliged to curb her art when the doctor told Albert to eat less
rich food, was one of the reasons for Nelly's growing resent-
ment. It had culminated in Albert's throwing his helping of
Christmas pudding at the wall.

Another factor, of course, was the oil man. He was not
every woman's idea of an attractive man, but his sleek black
hair and dark beard appealed to Nelly. He had a glib tongue
too, and was adept at flattery. It did not need much to woo
Nelly away from her husband, and she went to join him with
every confidence.

She saw now that his charms were superficial. She had never
been so short of money in her life, and she strongly suspected
that there were several other women in his life.

Things had gone from bad to worse, and one solitary
evening, as she ironed her companion's shirts, she worked out
just how little he gave her for housekeeping, and how much
she had been obliged to subtract from her Post Office account
during her stay. The results frightened her.

Here she was, getting on, not likely to get a job easily, and no future with Charlie as far as she could see. He was a bad bargain. The best thing to do was to cut her losses, return to Thrush Green, where she was more likely to get a job, and to throw herself on Albert's mercy – at least for a time. After all, she was his lawful wedded wife, and plenty of husbands had to turn a blind eye to their wives' little weaknesses, Nelly told herself.

Nelly was a realist. She finished the ironing, and went upstairs to pack. The next day she left a note for Charlie, collected some useful groceries from the larder, including a couple of chops which would do nicely for Albert's supper, and made her way to the station.

'Once I've got Albert sweet,' she thought to herself, as she faced the steep hill to Thrush Green, 'I'll pop along to Miss Watson and see if my old job's still open. If not, she'll know someone who could do with a bit of cleaning, I don't doubt.'

Puffing heavily, Nelly Piggott returned to Thrush Green.

On the morning after Ella's party, Winnie Bailey, the doctor's widow, made her way next door to Tullivers.

The May sunshine gilded the green. Daisies spangled the grass, and a lark's song fell from the blue, as clear and pure as a cascade of mountain water. How Donald loved a day like this, thought Winnie, tapping at the door. But there was no point in grieving. It was the last thing he would have wanted, and since his death she had learnt to savour each day as it came, to count her many blessings, and to try to put sadness behind her.

Phyllida and Frank Hurst had helped enormously, she

thought. What a comfort good neighbours could be!

Phil's head appeared at a bedroom window above her. 'Oh, do just walk in, Winnie dear. I'm coming down now.'

'I promised you some pansy plants,' said Winnie. 'I haven't brought them in case it's a busy time for you, but they're all ready next door whenever you need them.'

'Lovely!' said Phil. 'Come in and sit down, or shall we sit in the garden?'

'The garden,' said Winnie. 'It's much too gorgeous to stay indoors.'

They sat on the garden seat, facing the sun. A border of pinks nearby was beginning to break into flower, and the roses were in bud.

'You are going to have a fine show this summer,' commented Winnie.

'I know. The sad thing is that we shall miss most of it this year.'

'Not leaving Thrush Green?'

'Good heavens, no! But we only heard this morning that Jeremy and I can go with Frank to America in June.'

'The lecture tour you told me about?'

'That's right. It was all arranged, as you know, last autumn for Frank, but getting accommodation for Jeremy and me was the difficulty. Now we've heard that a publishing friend in Boston can put us up for the whole three months, if need be, or part of that time. I didn't think it right to drag Jeremy from place to place, but this arrangement will be perfect. Isn't it marvellous news?'

'It is indeed. And don't forget that I shall look forward to keeping an eye on the place for you.'

'You are kind. And Harold has offered to keep the garden in trim, so we feel that we can go with an easy conscience.'

'I hope you'll let me look after the cat too. She'll be much happier staying at Tullivers, I'm sure, and anyway she knows she is welcome next door if she feels lonely.'

'I *was* going to ask you about that,' admitted Phil. 'As a matter of fact, she virtually lives in the garden in the summer, so that she shouldn't be too much of a bother.'

Winnie rose to go.

'Now I must do some telephoning. Ella first. What a good party that was! I do hope Isobel finds a house soon. She'll be a great asset to Thrush Green, won't she?'

'Indeed she will. I heard her say that she intended to see if Williams and Frobisher have anything on their books. They're pretty reliable. What about her present house? Is it the sort that will sell easily?'

'I gather so. An ideal family house in a nice part of Sussex, and with a good train service to London. It should find plenty of buyers.'

'Well, I wish her joy of moving,' said Phil. 'It nearly killed me looking at houses and trying to sell the old one, all at the same time. It's usually so horribly *urgent*. People dying to get in before you are ready to get out, while you are waiting to see the colour of their money, and wondering if you can possibly afford all the alterations you will need in the new place. Heavens, what a terrible undertaking! I'm *never* going to move again!'

'And I'm delighted to hear it!' replied Winnie as she took her leave.

*   *   *

Betty Bell, Harold Shoosmith's voluble daily help, found her employer remarkably vague in manner that morning. She began to wonder if he had heard all the titbits of news which she enjoyed imparting.

'I was saying,' she repeated loudly, flicking a feather duster over Harold's treasured Coalport cottages, 'as Miss Fogerty's

a different person now her friend's here. They was always close, you know, ever since they was young girls, and Mrs Fletcher don't act no different now she's rich, to what she did before.'

Harold, now listening, felt some impatience. Why must gossip fly as soon as a newcomer appeared? It had been just the same when Phil Hurst had arrived.

'Why should she?' he commented shortly.

'Well, some does, you must allow,' replied Betty, glad to have his attention at last. 'And that Mrs Fletcher did do well for herself after all. Pots of money, and a husband as worshipped her—'

'I wish you wouldn't tittle-tattle so, Betty,' snapped Harold. 'No one's safe from gossips' tongues, it seems, at Thrush Green. I can well remember what poor Mrs Hurst had to endure when she first appeared here.'

Betty Bell's mouth dropped open in surprise, but she soon rallied, flicking the duster with alarming bravado.

'If you lives in a village, as you should know by now, new people gets talked about because they're *interesting*. Why, when you first come here I heard you'd been growing cocoa from Miss Ella, and coffee from Miss Dotty, and tea from Miss Dimity. And how many wives you'd had was nobody's business.'

'Good Lord!' exclaimed Harold, reeling from the attack.

'And what you'd *done* with them all kept everyone on tenterhooks, I can tell you,' went on Betty. 'So it's no good you trying to muzzle people in a village. They *likes* guessing about other people. It's better than a story in a book, or on the telly.'

'Yes, I do understand that, Betty, but I still think it is insufferable to pry into other people's affairs. Particularly unprotected people, like Mrs Fletcher who is still grieving for her husband.'

'She won't need to grieve for long,' said Betty shrewdly. 'She'll be snapped up by some man who's got eyes in his head and some sense too.'

She opened the door.

'Liver and bacon suit you? And a couple of tomatoes?'

'Lovely,' said Harold mechanically. It was funny, but his appetite seemed to have gone.

With Betty's departure to the kitchen, Harold set himself to the task of finishing the letters he had been writing before her arrival.

It was almost noon before he walked across Thrush Green to the post-box, his eyes straying towards Ella's house at the head of the hill.

He felt strangely disturbed by Betty's remarks about Isobel's probable remarriage. The damnable thing was that she was probably right in her forecast. She *was* an attractive woman, there was no doubt about it. The effect that handshake had had upon him was quite extraordinary. And yet she was completely without guile and those flirtatious ways which he so much detested in older women.

No, it would be no surprise to hear one day that she was going to marry. A very good thing, of course.

He dropped his letters in the box thoughtfully.

So why did he mind so much? He had only just met the woman, and yet she filled his mind. Did she remind him of earlier loves?

He thought of Daphne, fair and calm. And Lucy, who was a flirt and had married a fighter pilot who was killed. Then that red-haired minx, whose name he couldn't remember for the life of him, and her friend, who jolly nearly proposed to him when he wasn't on his guard.

At that moment, a car hooted, and there was the beautiful Alfa Romeo emerging from Ella's gate. Isobel saw him and waved.

With his heart pounding ('Like some fool boy of sixteen,' thought Harold crossly), he hurried along the road to greet her.

She held up a sheaf of papers.

'Williams and Frobisher are doing their stuff,' she told him. 'I picked these up this morning, and John Williams is taking me to see two houses south of Lulling.'

'Well done,' said Harold happily. The sun seemed extra warm and bright, the flowers twice as fragrant, and Isobel prettier than ever.

He patted the car.

'When you've time, would you tell me how you find this particular model? I think I shall have to change my car soon, and this looks as though it would suit me very well. How does it hold the road?'

'Very well indeed. I haven't had it long, but I tell you what. Why don't you drive it yourself? I want to look at another place somewhere between Minster Lovell and Burford tomorrow afternoon, and if you are free I should love to be driven, if you like the idea?'

'Like the idea! You adorable woman!' sang Harold's heart, but he heard himself thanking her politely and saying how very much he would like to try the car, and tomorrow afternoon was absolutely free, and he was entirely at her service.

'Then shall we say two o'clock tomorrow?' said Isobel,

giving him a smile which affected his heart in the most peculiar but delightful way. 'I'll hoot outside your gate.'

She waved, and drove off down the hill to Lulling, leaving Harold to cross the green on legs which had suddenly weakened.

'Here I am,' he said to himself in wonderment, 'in my sixties, a confirmed bachelor, and dammit, I'm in danger of falling in love!'

It was a disturbing thought. Another, even more disturbing, followed it.

'She'll hoot outside my gate at two o'clock! That'll make Thrush Green talk!'

He suddenly felt intensely happy, and went home, whistling.

The children at the village school were just emerging into the playground, after demolishing school dinner consisting of cold lamb and salad, pink blancmange and red jelly. They were, as always, in tearing high spirits and rushed about yelling happily, making such a fearful din that Miss Watson, who was on playground duty, only just heard the telephone ringing.

Agnes of course was in her new classroom across the playground, busy cutting up paper ready for her painting lesson that afternoon. The third teacher, a young probationer, would never dare to answer the telephone while her headmistress was at hand, so Miss Watson herself hurried round the side of the building to the lobby door.

Here stood a gigantic metal door-scraper which coped admirably in winter with the sticky Cotswold clay which the children brought along on their boots. In the summer, of course, it was scarcely needed, and Miss Watson had often thought that it should be taken up and stored somewhere during the fine months. It certainly constituted a hazard, and many a child had sustained a grazed knee by tripping over the thing.

On the other hand, where could it be stored? Like most old-fashioned village schools, Thrush Green's was short of outhouses and storage space in general. Such a large, rigid intractable object was impossible to store. Consequently, it remained *in situ* all the year.

In her haste, the telephone bell shrilling its urgency, poor Miss Watson caught her sensibly-shod foot against the edge of the scraper and fell sprawling into the lobby.

A few children hastened to her aid, and Miss Watson began to attempt to regain her feet and her dignity, but realised immediately that something was seriously amiss. It was going to be impossible to stand up. She began to feel faint.

'Get Miss Fogerty,' she told the children, as the playground whirled round and round amidst increasing darkness. The children fled towards the new classroom, and the young teacher appeared.

'Oh dear,' she cried. 'Here, let me help you up.'

She put strong arms about Miss Watson's shoulders and began to heave.

'No, no!' screamed poor Miss Watson. 'Don't move me, please.'

At that moment Agnes Fogerty arrived and took command, marshalling her memories of First Aid, learnt only last winter at Lulling.

'She's quite right,' she said. 'We mustn't move her. But quickly get her coat and a cushion, and then run across to Doctor Lovell.'

The girl fled, and Agnes knelt beside her head-mistress.

'Poor Dorothy,' she said, all thoughts of protocol vanishing in her anxiety. 'We're getting help. We'll soon have you more comfortable.'

She took the coat and cushion from her fellow teacher, covered the prone form and tucked the cushion gently under Miss Watson's head. Her face was very pale and her eyes were closed, but she managed to smile her thanks.

Fortunately, Doctor Lovell was still at his surgery, and hurried across. Within minutes he had rung for an ambulance, put the patient into a more comfortable position, and compli-mented Agnes on her grasp of the situation.

'They'll have to take her to Dickie's,' he said, using the local term for St Richard's Hospital in the county town. 'They've got all the right equipment there, X-rays and so on. It's the hip joint all right. One thing, they've some marvellous chaps there to put it right.'

Miss Fogerty would have liked to have accompanied her old friend to the hospital, but she knew where her duty lay.

'I'll come and see you as soon as possible,' she promised, as the stretcher was put into the ambulance, and Miss Watson nodded wanly.

'Mind the school,' she managed to whisper, as the doors shut.

Agnes watched the ambulance until it vanished down the hill and turned back, shaken in body, but resolute in spirit, to carry out her headmistress's last command.

12 House-Hunting

WHEN Nelly Piggott finally arrived at her own doorstep, she dropped her heavy case and grocery carrier and paused to take breath.

The brass door handle, she noticed, was badly tarnished, the step itself, thick with footmarks. Behind the sparse wallflowers was lodged a collection of crisp bags, ice-lolly sticks and cigarette cartons which had blown there from the public house next door, and which Albert had failed to remove.

Time I was home, thought Nelly to herself, and opened the door.

'What's going on?' growled Albert thickly. 'Who's that, eh? Get on off!'

There was the sound of a chair being shifted, and Albert still muttering, approached. Nelly swiftly heaved her luggage inside and followed it nimbly, shutting the door behind her.

Albert confronted her. His eyes and mouth were round Os of astonishment, but he soon found his voice.

'None of that, my girl! You're not comin' back here, I'm tellin' you. Clear orf! Go on, you baggage, clear orf, I say!'

He began to advance upon her, one threatening fist upraised, but Nelly took hold of his thin shoulders, and guided him swiftly backwards towards the chair. He sat down with a grunt, and was immediately overtaken by a prolonged fit of coughing.

Nelly stood over him, watching until the paroxysm spent itself.

'Yes, well, you see what happens when you lose your temper,' she said calmly. There was a hint of triumph in her voice which enraged Albert. He struggled to rise, but Nelly put him down again with one hand.

'Just you be reasonable, Albert Piggott.'

'*Reasonable!*' choked Albert. 'You walks out! You comes back! You expects me to welcome you, as though nothink 'as 'appened? You can go back to that so-and-so. Or 'as he chucked you out?'

'Certainly not,' said Nelly, putting the carrier bag on the table, and feeling for the chops. 'I came of my own accord.'

'Oh, did you? Well, you can dam' well go back of your own accord.'

Nelly changed her tactics.

'You may not like it, Albert Piggott, but you'll have to lump it. Here I am, and here I stay, at least for the night, and you can thank your stars as I've brought you some nice chops for your supper. From the look of you, you can do with a square meal.'

Albert lay back. Exhaustion kept him from answering, but the thought of a return to Nelly's cooking, however brief, was a pleasant one.

Nelly began to busy herself about the kitchen, and Albert watched her through half-closed eyes.

'And when did this place last get a scrub up?'

'Molly done it lovely,' whispered Albert, defending his family.

'And not been touched since,' said Nelly tartly, filling the kettle. 'This frying-pan wants a good going over before it's fit for use.'

She whisked about, unpacking the chops, and some tomatoes and onions. For all his fury, Albert could not help feeling some slight pleasure at the sight of her at her old familiar ploys. He roused himself.

'Seein' as you've pushed yourself in, you'd best stay the night, I suppose. But it'll have to be the spare bed. You ain't comin' in with me.'

'Don't flatter yourself,' said Nelly shortly, investigating dripping in a stone jamjar.

She scoured the pan, and then set the food into it. Once the cooking had begun to her satisfaction, she took up the heavy case and began to mount the stairs.

Albert heard her thumping about above. The fragrant smells of frying onion and chops wreathed about the kitchen, and Albert settled back in his chair with a happy sigh.

As Harold Shoosmith had foreseen, a number of interested spectators focused their attention on the Alfa Romeo at his gate on the afternoon in question. He felt more amusement than embarrassment as Isobel emerged elegantly from the driver's seat, and let him take her place.

They drove slowly along the chestnut avenue in front of the Youngs' house and then turned right to descend the hill. The sun was warm and the flowering cherries were beginning to break into a froth of pink in the gardens which faced south.

They headed westward through the outskirts of the town and were soon on the windy heights. On their right lay the valley of the Windrush, its meandering course marked by willow trees already showing tender leaves of greenish gold.

'Heavenly afternoon,' commented Isobel. Harold agreed. It was not only the balmy spring weather which made it heavenly for him. Isobel's presence was the main source of his contentment, but he had to admit that the smooth performance of the little car also contributed to his pleasure.

'Can we spare time to drop down to Minster Lovell?' he asked. 'If the Swan still does teas we could call on our way back, if you'd like that?'

'Very much, thank you. But I think we'll be lucky to find anywhere that provides teas these days. Isn't it sad? Tea's such a nice meal.'

'My favourite. After breakfast,' smiled Harold.

They took a turning to the right, and ran down the hill to Minster Lovell. Harold stopped the car outside the beautiful old pub, and got out to speak to a woman who was cleaning the windows.

'No, dear,' she said. 'No call for teas much. And it's getting staff as is difficult. Besides, people don't want tea these days.'

'We do,' said Harold.

'Ah well, dear, "Want must be your master", as my old gran used to say. You going near Burford? You'd get some there, no doubt. You see, there's coaches and that, pulling up there, and there's more call for teas then.'

Harold thanked her, and returned to the car.

'I think,' said Isobel dreamily, 'that is one of the loveliest villages in England. How I long to get back here! Sussex is beautiful, but it's here I belong.'

'Then we'd better push on to see this house,' said Harold practically, letting in the clutch.

It was not easy to find. The little blue car nosed its way through narrow lanes, between steep banks starred with late primroses and early stitchwort. They passed sign posts to Burford, to Astall Leigh, to Swinbrook, to Witney, and were beginning to wonder if the house really existed when they saw the 'For Sale' sign.

The house was built on the side of a hill, and a steep path went from the lane to the front door. It was a substantial dwelling of honey-gold Cotswold stone, and a scarlet japonica covered the side wall.

'Would you like to come in?' asked Isobel.

'I won't, many thanks,' said Harold. 'It's easier for you to ask questions, and take in what the owners tell you, if you are on your own. I'll wait a little farther down the road, where it is wider.'

'Fine,' said Isobel, collecting her bag and papers. Obviously she was expected, for at that moment the front door opened, and a woman peered out.

Harold watched the two meet, and then drove to the arranged parking place. Here he got out, leant upon a conveniently sited five-barred gate, and surveyed the pleasant scene spread out below him.

He could well understand Isobel's longing to return. His own affection for the area grew with every year that passed. He had never regretted, for one instant, his decision to settle at Thrush Green. He had made many new friends, not an easy thing to accomplish when one was a middle-aged new-comer to a small community, and the countryside was a constant delight.

His own domestic arrangements were also satisfying, although of late he had begun to wonder if the years ahead would prove lonely. He had never regretted his bachelor state. After all, it was of his own choosing, and very contented he had been with it. But observing the happiness of the rector, Charles Henstock, in his second marriage, had given Harold cause for thought.

Not that one should contemplate matrimony solely for the betterment of one's lot. Such selfishness would be a sure way to disaster. A true marriage, to Harold's mind, should be a joyous partnership, and if it were not to be so then it were better to remain single.

He had a healthy distrust of strong emotions, and viewed his own present disturbance with mingled amusement, pleasure and caution. But he recognised a deeper feeling towards Isobel which he felt that time would confirm. He hoped that she would soon be living nearby, and that time would prove him right as he grew to know her.

He walked down the lane between the hawthorn hedges shining with new leaf. The sun was warm, some lambs gam-bolled in the water meadow below, and a thrush sang as it bounced on a flowering spray of blackthorn above him.

When he returned, Isobel was waiting in the car.

'Any luck?' he asked, as he climbed into the driver's seat.

Isobel shook her head.

'Too much needs to be done. It would cost a fortune. And it's dark, and faces north-east. A pity, because the rooms were nice, and my stuff would have looked well there.'

Harold patted her hand.

'Never mind, there'll be others.'

'But I haven't much time. Only two more days. I think I must try and come again later on, when I've sorted things out at home.'

'Must you go this week?'

'I'm afraid so. There are various bits of business to attend to in the next two or three weeks, and I certainly hope to have a few offers for my house to consider.'

Harold nodded. At least it was some comfort to know that she planned to return in the near future.

'Will you stay with Ella again?'

'No, I think not. It's not really fair to her. There's the Fleece, though I'm not keen on staying at hotels. The evenings drag so. But don't let's bother about all that now. Who knows what the next two days may bring? And anyway, what about that cup of tea?'

'Burford may be crowded. What about having tea with me? I can offer you Earl Grey, or Lapsang Souchong, or plain Indian.'

'The last will suit me beautifully,' replied Isobel, with a smile which turned Harold's heart somersaulting.

'Thrush Green it is then,' he replied, letting in the clutch. And the conversation on their homeward way consisted exclusively of the merits, or otherwise, of the Alfa Romeo.

Dotty Harmer, with Flossie in tow, had just delivered the goat's milk to Ella, when they both noticed Isobel's car outside Harold's gate.

'They must be back,' said Ella, stating the obvious. 'I wonder if she's had any luck today?'

'But why is she at Harold's?'

'Search me,' said Ella carelessly. 'Popped in to borrow a map or a book, I daresay. She may be staying with me for a week, Dotty dear, but that doesn't mean she's not free to visit whenever and whoever she pleases.'

Dotty ruminated, her hand stroking Flossie's satin head.

'But why *Harold*?'

'He was trying out her car, that's why. And now, Dotty, to business. I've been paying you five peas for years now. I'm sure the milk should be more. That hogwash from the dairy— so-called—has gone up about six times since we fixed things. What about eight peas?'

'Is that more than a shilling?'

'Lord, yes! More like one and six.'

'Then I refuse to take it. One shilling is ample, Ella. I really wish this pea business had never started. There are so many things I find that muddle me today. Metres and litres and grammes. So bewildering. And what's all this voluntary aided tax I keep finding on my bills?'

'*Taxes*,' replied Ella severely, 'are neither voluntary nor aided, as you should well know! VAT stands for *value added tax*.'

Dotty considered the information, her eyes fixed unseeingly on the distant Alfa Romeo.

'If anything,' she remarked at last, 'it sounds sillier.'

Ella rummaged in her purse and handed Dotty a silver fivepenny piece.

'It's not enough, Dotty, but if that's how you want it—'

'It is indeed. I put all the goat's milk money in a special tobacco tin, and it's surprising how it mounts up. I bought a large bag of dog biscuits with it last time, for dear old Floss.'

'Well, she looks pretty fit on it,' agreed Ella, opening the gate for her departing friend.

Dotty hurried away across the green, her stockings in wrinkles as usual and the hem of her petticoat showing a good two inches below her skirt.

Ella watched her go with affection, and turned to carry in the milk. Her eye was caught by Isobel's car again.

'Quite old enough to know what she's doing,' thought Ella, 'and anyway, none of my business.'

Not all the Thrush Green residents were as tolerant.

Bob Jones, landlord of the Two Pheasants noticed that the dashing blue car was over an hour outside Harold's house, and to his mind, 'it looked bad'. What if Mr Shoosmith and Mrs Fletcher were both middle-aged? Also, they were both unattached, and it was indiscreet, to say the least, to lay themselves open to comment.

Winnie Bailey's faithful maid Jenny also noticed the car and, although she said nothing, she pursed her mouth primly as she set about some ironing in her top flat. Winnie herself was incapable of distinguishing Isobel's car from the milkman's delivery van, and so remained unperturbed by the private tea party.

Albert Piggott was probably the most censorious, but since Nelly's return he was in such a state of turmoil, and his indigestion seemed so much worse, now that he was tempted by Nelly's rich food, that it was not surprising.

'No better than she should be,' he told Nelly. 'I could see she be a proper flighty one as soon as I set eyes on that flashy car of hers.'

'Well, I don't know the lady,' said Nelly roundly, 'but I knows Thrush Green and the tongues as wags round it. I'll bet my bottom dollar she's as innocent as I am.'

'As you are!' echoed Albert derisively. 'Some innocent! And talking of that, when are you gettin' back to that Charlie you're so fond of?'

Nelly folded a tea towel with care.

'See here, Albert. Let's jog on a bit longer, shall we? I've said I'm sorry for that last little upset and you know you needs a woman in this place. What about me stoppin' on and gettin'

my old job back? I thought I might call on Miss Watson this evening.'

Albert snorted.

'Then you'll have a long way to go, my gal. She's in Dickie's with a broken leg or summat. It'll be Miss Fogerty in charge now, and for all I knows Betty Bell's doin' the cleanin', and makin' a good job of it too.'

Nelly did her best to look unconcerned at this unwelcome piece of news.

'No harm in asking anyway,' she said, tossing her head. 'Maybe Miss Fogerty'd preter me to Betty Bell. I always done my best at the school before, and Miss Watson told me so. "Never seen it so clean," was her very words.'

'Go your own way,' growled Albert. 'You will anyway, but don't come grizzling to me when you find there ain't no job there for you, my gal.'

He hobbled to the door, took down his greasy cap from the peg, and began his journey across to the church.

The Alfa Romeo gleamed in the afternoon sunshine, and Albert saw Isobel emerge from Harold's front door closely followed by her host. They both looked extremely happy.

'The baggage!' muttered Albert.

He picked up a clod of earth from the church porch.

'Women!' he added viciously.

He threw the clod spitefully towards an adjacent tomb stone, and was mollified to see that it bespattered one 'Alice, Dutiful Wife and Mother, An Example of Pious Womanhood'.

'Women!' repeated Albert, opening the church door. 'All the same! Dead or living. All the same!'

13 Miss Fogerty Carries On

MISS FOGERTY rang the hospital in the early evening expecting to hear that her headmistress was either 'comfortable', which no one could be in Miss Watson's condition, or 'as well as could be expected', which was one of those ominous expressions guaranteed to set one choosing hymns for the funeral.

But to her surprise a remarkably kind sister answered the telephone and assured Miss Fogerty that the patient had stood the operation well, and that, although she had not yet come round, she would be certain to enjoy a visit the next evening.

'Can you tell me,' asked Miss Fogerty diffidently, 'I mean, are you *allowed* to tell me, exactly what was wrong?'

One did not wish such a nice woman to break the oath of Hippocrates, if, of course, she had ever had to take one, but one really must know more.

'A dislocated hip joint, with some damage,' said the sister. 'These days it's quite simple to pop it back.'

She made it sound as easy as returning a cork to a bottle top, but Miss Fogerty shuddered sympathetically in the telephone box.

'Thank you for telling me,' she said sincerely. 'Please give her my love. Just say "Agnes rang". And I will call tomorrow evening.'

While she was there, she telephoned to Miss Watson's brother and left a message with his wife. She seemed an emotional woman, and her voice came wailing down the line.

'Oh dear, what a catastrophe! What will Ray say? I'll tell him the minute he gets in. He's so devoted to Dorothy. I expect he'll want her to come here as soon as she's out of hospital, and I really can't see —'

The wailing died away.

'That's looking rather far ahead,' said little Miss Fogerty. 'But let me give you the hospital's number, and then you can keep in touch.'

That done, she rang off, and went across to the schoolhouse to make sure that all was locked up safely.

It did not look as though poor Dorothy would have her convalescence with her brother.

'And probably all for the best,' thought Miss Fogerty. 'She'll be better off in her own home.'

Ella Bembridge said goodbye to Isobel after breakfast one sunny morning.

She watched the little blue car descend the hill, gave one last wave, and turned back to the empty house.

'I'm going to miss her,' thought Ella, fumbling for the tobacco tin which housed the materials for making cigarettes.

She sat on the window seat and surveyed the view across Thrush Green, as she rolled herself a cigarette.

The house was very quiet. A frond of young honeysuckle tapped against the window, moved rhythmically by the light breeze. Ella drew in a satisfying lungful of tobacco smoke, and exhaled luxuriously.

'Quiet, but nice,' she said aloud. 'After all, it's what I'm used to. Nothing like a bit of solitude now and again.'

The sound of a door shutting made her swivel round. Dimity was coming across from the rectory, and Ella stumped to the front door to welcome her.

'Don't say she's gone!' exclaimed Dimity, surveying the empty drive. 'I thought Isobel said "after lunch".'

'After *breakfast*,' replied Ella.

'What a pity! I'd brought her a pot of my bramble jelly.'

'Well, ten chances to one she'll be back again in a few weeks.'

'Staying here?'

'I'd like her to, but from one or two things she said, I think she'll put up at the Fleece. Seems to think it's *imposing* on me, or some such nonsense.'

'She's a very considerate person,' said Dimity. 'We're going to miss her.'

Betty Bell echoed these sentiments as she attacked Harold's kitchen sink.

'I see Mrs Fletcher's gone home. Miss Fogerty will miss her, though no doubt she's got enough to do with that school on her hands. Pretty woman, isn't she?'

'Who?' asked Harold, purposely obtuse.

'Why, Mrs Fletcher! Mind you, it's partly her clothes. Always dressed nice, she did. That's what money does, of course. It's nice for her to have a bit put by, even if she does marry again.'

Harold snorted, and made for the door. This everlasting tittle-tattling was too irritating to bear. As he gained the peace

of his hall, he saw the rector at the door, and gladly invited
him in.

'I've just come from Ella's,' said Charles, 'and she's given
me Isobel's address. She thought you might want it.'

Harold was taken aback.

'Isobel's address?'

'In case you heard of a house, I think Ella said. I know she's
got the estate agent working here, but really bush telegraph
sometimes works so much more swiftly, and who knows?
You *may* hear of something.'

'Of course, of course,' replied Harold, collecting himself.
'Ella will miss her, I expect.'

'A truly *womanly* woman,' commented the rector. 'Who
was it said: "I like a manly man, and a womanly woman, but
I can't bear a boily boy"?'

'No idea,' said Harold. 'Have a drink?'

'No, no, my dear fellow. I have a confirmation class this
evening, and must go and prepare a few notes. And there's
poor Jacob Bly's funeral at two, and Dimity wants me to help
sort out the boots and shoes for the jumble sale.'

Harold was instantly reminded of another parson, James
Woodforde, who had written in his diary, two hundred years
earlier, of just such an incongruous collection of activities in
one day. The duties of a parson, it seemed, embraced many
interests as well as the care of the living and the dead, no matter
in which century he lived.

'Then I won't keep you,' said Harold. 'Thank you for the
address, and if I hear of anything I shall get in touch with
Isobel, of course, although I think that the chances are
slight.'

Little did he realise that he would be invited to write to the
address in his hand, within a few days.

Agnes Fogerty was indeed too busy to miss dear Isobel as
sorely as she might have done.

She was now Acting Headmistress, a role which filled her
with more misgiving than pride.

Apart from the day to day responsibilities, there was a
profusion of forms from the office which had to be completed
and returned, 'without delay' as the headings stated with
severity. Agnes, conscious of her duties, spent many an evening
struggling with them in her bed-sitting room.

Then there was the supply teacher sent by the office to help
during Miss Watson's absence.

Miss Fogerty found her unnerving, and her discipline non-
existent. It worried Agnes to see the children talking when
they should have been working. She disliked the way Miss
Enderby's charges wandered freely about the classroom, in
theory collecting their next piece of work, in practice giving a
sly clout to anyone in their path. Either Miss Enderby did not
see what was going on, which was reprehensible, or she *did*
see and condoned it, which was worse. Eventually, Agnes
spoke of the matter and had great chunks of some dreadful
report or other quoted to her. To Agnes, the report seemed
quite irrelevant to the matter in hand, but Miss Enderby
seemed to cling so fiercely to the findings of whatever-
committee-it-was responsible for this half-inch thick treatise
that Agnes decided to retire temporarily from the field of
battle. No doubt there would be other occasions when a word
of advice could be offered.

There were. There were many occasions, and brave little Miss Fogerty did her best to put things politely but firmly. She found Miss Enderby's attitude quite mystifying. Throughout her teaching career, Miss Fogerty had worked on the principle that children did as they were told. One did not ask them to do anything *impossible*, of course, or *wrong*, or *beyond their powers*. But open defiance, or the complete ignoring of orders given, had never been countenanced in Agnes's classroom, and all had gone on swimmingly.

What was the good, Agnes asked herself, in reading all those papers and reports with terrible titles like: 'The Disruptive Child and Its Place In Society' or 'Where Have Teachers Gone Wrong?' if at the end of it one still could not *teach*? It was quite apparent that the class now under Miss Enderby's care (one could not say 'control') had learned practically nothing since her advent. That it was dear Miss Watson's class made it even worse.

Miss Enderby, it was clear, was a theorist, but one quite incapable of putting theories into practice. The children would not allow it. They were having a field day enjoying themselves without stricture. In a rare flash of insight, Agnes Fogerty saw that her unsatisfactory supply teacher clung to the theories which she so avidly imbibed, and quoted, because they were all that she had to get her through each day's teaching.

Agnes prayed nightly for her headmistress's return to health and Thrush Green School. She was to come home from the hospital after a fortnight, and Agnes had offered, very diffidently, to stay at the schoolhouse if it would help.

'It is more than kind of you, Agnes dear,' Dorothy had

said, 'but I expect Ray will want me to convalesce with them. I shall see him one evening this week.'

Agnes had murmured something non-committal, and repeated her willingness to help in any way, but Dorothy seemed to be quite sure that she would be looked after by her brother and his wife.

'I wonder,' thought Agnes, hurrying through driving rain to the bus stop. 'Poor dear Dorothy! I wonder!'

Robert Bassett made slow but steady progress after his second attack, but it was quite apparent that his confidence was shaken.

'He's suddenly become an old man,' said Joan sadly. 'I hate to see it. He doesn't look ahead as he always did. All the *spunk* seems to have gone out of the poor old boy.'

She was talking to her brother-in-law, John Lovell, after one of his visits to the patient.

'It's nature's way of making him rest. You'll see, he'll pick up before long. Meanwhile, there's one good thing to emerge from this setback.'

'And what's that?'

'He's quite given up the idea of going back to the business, and that's as it should be. In a way, I think he's glad that this blow has settled things for him. He's now coming to terms with the idea.'

'He said as much to mother, I know, but he hasn't said anything very definite to us. I believe he worries in case we feel that he wants his own house back!'

'If I were you,' said John, 'I should broach the subject yourselves. Tell him Edward's plans for the conversion, and let him toy with the idea. I believe it will do him good to have something to look forward to and to occupy his mind.'

After this conversation, Joan and Edward took John's advice, and spoke frankly about their plans to the parents. Milly had known what was afoot for days, but to Robert it came as a complete surprise.

To the Youngs' delight, he seemed excited and pleased at the ideas put forward, and studied Edward's rough sketches with enthusiasm.

'Leave them with me, dear boy,' he said. 'Milly and I will have a proper look at them, and we may even make one or two suggestions. I can see that you two have been hatching up this little plot for some time, and I am really very touched.'

He smiled a little tremulously, and Joan rose swiftly to put him at his ease.

'I'm off to find us something to eat. Come and give me a hand, Edward,' she said, making for the door.

'Bless his old heart,' said Edward, when they reached the kitchen. 'He's as pleased as Punch! How I like satisfied clients!'

'Don't speak too soon,' warned Joan, busy at the stove. 'He may not be satisfied. Besides, he's every right to turn us out, you know.'

'He won't,' said Edward, dropping a basket of bread rolls on the floor, and bending to retrieve them. 'He's the most unselfish soul alive.'

He picked up the rolls, dusted each down the side of his trousers, and put them carefully in the basket again.

Her husband, thought Joan, might be a talented architect, but his grasp of culinary hygiene was nil.

In the Piggotts' household an uneasy truce was being carried on.

Nelly was content to live from day to day, gradually cleaning the cottage until it satisfied her own high standards, and cooking succulent meals which Albert secretly enjoyed. Wild horses would not have dragged thanks from him, under the circumstances, and the frequent bouts of indigestion which attacked him kept him as morose as usual.

There was no doubt about it, thought Nelly, as she attacked the filthy cooker one afternoon with plenty of hot soda water, Albert did not improve with age. As soon as she could get a job, she would be off again. But jobs, it seemed, were hard to find.

She had called on her old friends at the Drovers' Arms, but they were already well-staffed, and in any case were not inclined to do anything to upset Albert. She had come back of her own accord, they felt, and it was up to her to do what she could to look after the old man, curmudgeonly though he might be. Work at the Drovers' Arms meant that Nelly would be away from home for a considerable part of the day.

Undeterred by the news that Betty Bell now cleaned the school, Nelly called one evening at Miss Fogerty's lodgings.

Mrs White, Miss Fogerty's landlady, opened the door, and was somewhat taken aback by the flamboyant figure on the doorstep. She knew quite well who the visitor was, but as she strongly disapproved of Nelly, and her morals, she feigned ignorance.

'Someone to see you, Miss Fogerty,' she called up the stairs. 'If you would like to go up?' she said to Nelly, standing back against the flowery wallpaper.

Miss Fogerty looked even more alarmed than her landlady

had been at first sight of Nelly puffing up the stairs. She showed her into her bed-sitting room, and closed the door.

Nelly, seating herself in the only comfortable armchair, looked about her. She noticed the faded carpet, the thin curtains, and the bedspread which was not quite large enough to cover the divan bed. But she noticed too, in that first swift glance, that everything was clean—beautifully clean.

The furniture was well polished, the shabby paintwork and the mottled tiles of the hearth were spotless. Miss Fogerty's small array of toilet things stood in a tidy row on a glass shelf over the corner wash-basin. Her books stood neatly, row by row in the bedside bookcase. Only a pile of exercise books, in the process of being marked, gave any clue to the present activity in Miss Fogerty's modest abode.

On the mantel shelf stood two shining brass candlesticks, one at each end. A china cat stood by one, and a china spaniel by the other. A small travelling clock stood dead centre, and on each side stood a photograph.

One showed Miss Fogerty's shoemaker father looking stern. His right hand rested on the shoulder of his wife, sitting on an ornately carved chair in front of him. Agnes's mother looked meek and submissive. Her hair was parted in the middle. Her eyes were downcast. Her hands were folded in the centre of her lap. A fine aspidistra at the side of the couple seemed to display far more vitality than the photographer's sitters.

But it was the second photograph which engaged Nelly's attention. It was framed in silver, and showed the likeness of a fair young man in army uniform. He was smiling, showing excellent teeth, and he wore his hair *en brosse*. Could he be a sweetheart, Nelly wondered? Could colourless, shabby little Miss Fogerty ever have inspired love in someone so obviously lively? You never knew, of course. Still waters ran deep . . . She looked from the photograph to her reluctant hostess, who was now seated in an uncomfortable chair which she had turned round from the dressing table.

'I expect you are wondering why I've come,' began Nelly, removing her scarf.

'Naturally,' replied Miss Fogerty with truth, and just a touch of hauteur. She disliked Nelly, and had never been happy about her appointment as cleaner at the school. She accepted the fact that Nelly was excellent at her job, but she thought her a vulgar creature and not a suitable person to be

among young children. She had deplored the fact that it was
Miss Watson who had taken on Nelly, and could only put it
down to her headmistress's kind heart, and the paucity of
applicants for the post at that time.

'Well, I was hoping that my old job might be going still.
Always enjoyed it, I did, and I know Miss Watson was
satisfied. Pity she's away. Is she going on all right?'

'Yes, thank you,' said Agnes shortly. She did not propose
to discuss dear Dorothy's condition with this woman. 'And
the post is already filled, Mrs Piggott. Betty Bell is with us now,
so that I'm afraid I can't help you.'

'She suit you all right? That Betty Bell?'

'Perfectly,' said Agnes firmly. She rose to indicate that the
meeting was ended, but Nelly remained firmly wedged in
the armchair.

'I hear she works at Mr Shoosmith's too,' she remarked.
'I wonder she finds time to do two jobs. *Properly*, that is!'

The implications of this snide observation were not lost
upon Agnes. Really, the woman was insufferable, and there
were all those essays waiting to be marked, and her hair to
wash, and the hem of her skirt to be repaired where she had
caught it as she had tidied the bottom of the handwork cupboard. What a nuisance Nelly Piggott was, to be sure!

'She is a very hard-working girl,' said Miss Fogerty sharply,
'and manages her various jobs excellently. Not only does she go
to Mr Shoosmith, I think you'll find she helps Miss Harmer
as well, and we are all quite satisfied with her work.'

Agnes remained standing, and Nelly, facing defeat, struggled
from the armchair.

'Wouldn't take much to satisfy Miss Harmer from what I

hear,' said Nelly, 'but there it is. If there's nothing I can do at the school, I'll have to look elsewhere.'

She began to arrange the scarf around her fourth chin.

'Don't know of anyone, I suppose, as needs help?'

'I'm afraid not,' replied Agnes, a trifle less frostily now that she saw her visitor departing. She opened the door to the landing and ushered Nelly through it.

'Well, if you do hear of anything you know where I live,' said Nelly, descending the stairs heavily.

'I will bear it in mind,' promised Agnes, now opening the front door.

'Ta ever so, dearie,' said Nelly, sailing down the path.

Shuddering, Miss Fogerty returned to her interrupted peace.

14 Comings and Goings

IT was Charles Henstock who first told Harold Shoosmith that Phil was accompanying Frank on his trip to the United States.

'I knew Frank was off, and said I'd keep an eye on the garden for him, but I didn't realise that Phil could go too. Do them both good to have a change, and Jeremy will enjoy being off school.'

'They come back early in September, so the boy won't miss much,' replied Charles. 'It will be strange to see Tullivers empty.'

'Empty!' echoed Harold, a splendid idea bourgeoning. He decided to visit Frank and Phil Hurst that very evening, and found them in the garden when he did so.

June had come in with what the Irish call 'soft weather'. Skies were overcast, but the air was mild and the wind gentle. Frank's roses were beginning to make a fine show, and both he and Phil were hoeing round the bushes.

They put down their tools to greet Harold.

'Don't let me stop you,' he said.

'Thank God you've come, and given us an excuse to have a break,' replied Frank feelingly. 'I'll get drinks.'

He vanished into the house, and Harold and Phil seated themselves on the grass. A robin, matchstick legs askew, watched them with his head on one side.

'I suppose you realise that you are doing that poor chap out of his worm supper, now that you've stopped hoeing?'

'He's had enough already,' said Phil. 'It's a wonder he doesn't pop.'

Frank arrived with the drinks.

'Heard that Phil and Jeremy are coming with me?' asked Frank, smiling.

'I have indeed. Wonderful news. Charles told me.'

'So we'll be even more glad than before to know you are keeping an eye on things,' said Frank. 'I don't like leaving the place empty, but there it is. Luckily, we've got good neighbours, like you and Winnie, to look out for any baddies around.'

Harold put down his drink carefully.

'It's that really which brings me over this evening.'

'How do you mean? Are you going away too?'

'No. I shall be here. I just wondered if you would consider Isobel Fletcher having the house for part of the time. She intends to come back towards the end of June, I gather, unless she's fixed up beforehand.'

'Sounds splendid,' said Phil enthusiastically. 'But would she want to be bothered?'

'Frankly, I've no idea,' confessed Harold. 'It was just a thought. I know she doesn't want to impose on Ella any further, and doesn't particularly relish staying at an hotel. Anyway, perhaps it's cheek of me to suggest it.'

'Not at all,' said Frank heartily. 'I should feel much happier if someone were staying in the place, and I can't think of anyone more suitable. Shall we let you know definitely tomorrow?

Then you can get in touch with Isobel, or we will, if you'd rather we did.'

'That's fine,' agreed Harold. He picked up his glass with a satisfied sigh. 'Of course, she may have found something already, but I doubt it. It would be marvellous to have her here, right on the spot.'

Phil looked at his blissful expression with sudden awareness.

'So convenient for the house-hunting,' explained Harold hastily, 'and I'm sure she would be a most careful tenant while you are away.'

'It was a very good idea of yours,' said Frank, 'and now come and have a look at the jasmine you gave us. It's nearly reached the roof.'

Phil collected the glasses and carried them indoors.

'So that's how the land lies,' she said to herself. 'Now who would have thought it?'

Later that evening, when Jeremy was safely asleep upstairs, Phil told Frank about her suspicions. Predictably, he was scornful.

'Old Harold? And Isobel? Rubbish, my dear, you're imagining things! Why, I've known Harold for donkey's years, and he's always been the happiest of confirmed bachelors. He's not likely to change now. Why should he?'

'I don't suppose there's any particular *reason* why he should want to give up his bachelordom, but I'm sure I'm right about this. After all, you were getting on perfectly well on your own when we first met, but you embarked upon matrimony without a qualm.'

'That's different. You are a most attractive woman.'

'So is Isobel. I can quite understand Harold's change of heart.'

'You're incurably romantic, my darling. It comes of writing for all those women's magazines, I expect. So you are all in favour of enticing Isobel here to further the course of true love?'

'I am indeed. To be honest, that's only the secondary consideration. I'd like someone to be in the house basically.'

'And you've no scruples about leaving defenceless Isobel to Harold's amorous bombardment?'

It was Phil's turn to snort.

'I should think Harold's ardour has subsided to manageable levels in his sixties. And Isobel must have had plenty of experience in warding off unwanted suitors in her time.'

'So you think Harold will be unwanted? Poor old Harold!'

Phil reflected.

'I can't speak for Isobel, of course. She may not want to marry again. She has no family to consider now, and she has lots of friends and a comfortable income. She may well turn down any offer from Harold. That's the pity. I'm afraid he would be very upset.'

'I expect he's taken harder knocks than that in his time,' commented Frank.

'Maybe,' agreed his wife, 'but you know what Jane Austen said? "It is always incomprehensible to a man that a woman should ever refuse an offer of marriage".'

Frank laughed.

'I'll let you, or rather, Jane Austen, have the last word. One thing I've learnt in life is that a man is no match for a woman in affairs of this sort. So, we invite Isobel?'

'We invite Isobel,' agreed Phil.

The sun was slowly dispersing the clouds as Frank walked across to Harold's the next morning.

The chestnut avenue was now in full leaf, and the white and pink candles were in flower. Outside the Two Pheasants Bob Jones's hanging baskets made a brave show, the geraniums quite untouched by those frosts which Albert Piggott had forecast earlier.

A yellow Mermaid rose was in full bloom on the sunny side of Harold's house, and the borders on each side of his path glowed with violas, pinks and double daisies. It all looked remarkably spruce, thought Frank. Surely, Harold could want no more than this for happiness? He had made a perfect life for himself in the place of his choice. Was it likely that he would embark on the complications of married life?

He had no need to knock at the door, for Betty Bell, with Brasso and duster in hand, burst out as he approached.

'Lor!' she said, clutching the Brasso to her heart. 'You fair frit me, you did!'

'Sorry, Mrs Bell,' said Frank. 'Is Mr Shoosmith in?'

'Down the garden, by the bonfire. Shall I give him a holler for you?'

'No, no. I'll go and see him.'

Sure enough, Harold was tending a small bonfire, whose smoke was drifting in the leisurely breeze towards Lulling Woods. Looking at him, with his wife's surmises in mind, Frank had to admit that Harold was wearing very well, and was still remarkably good-looking.

And tidy too, thought Frank, a little enviously. Harold always looked immaculate, even when tackling a messy job, as he was doing now. He himself, Frank knew, would be crumpled and smeared with smuts, his hands black, and his gardening clothes deplorable. Phil despaired of him at times. She had often told him so.

Harold turned to replenish his fire and saw his old friend.

'Hallo, there! What's the news?'

'Unanimous approval of your bright idea! Will you get in touch with Isobel? Or shall we?'

Harold looked a trifle discomfited.

'I think you should deal with her directly, Frank. By all

means say I thought of it, if you like, but I'm sure it's best to have a word with her yourselves.'

'Very well. I'll write today, and perhaps she can ring me when she's studied the suggestion, and we can fix up things then.'

'Fine, fine!' replied Harold. He looked as though he might say more, thought better of it, and changed the subject.

'And when do you fly? Do you want a lift to the airport? I'm a free man, you know, and only too pleased to take you.'

'In just over a fortnight, and it would be marvellous if you can take us to Heathrow. You're sure about this?'

'Positive—or nearly so. Come inside, and we'll have a look at the diary. In any case, it will only be one or other of these dam' committees I seem to have dropped into. I shouldn't be missed.'

Betty Bell was busy setting out cups upon a tray as they went through the kitchen.

'I'm getting you two gents a nice cup of coffee,' she said. 'Here, or in the study?'

'In the study, Betty,' said Harold hastily. 'We've something to look up.'

When alone, Harold usually took his elevenses with Betty, allowing her incessant chatter to flow over him. Today he felt that it would not be fair to inflict all the local gossip on his old friend.

'Okey-doke,' said Betty, to their retreating backs.

The diary for the week in question read: Monday, Vestry meeting 7.0. Wednesday, Dentist 10.30. Scouts' Concert 7.30. Thursday, Remember B and B, Friday and Saturday were clear.

'I wonder what "Remember B and B" means?' pondered Harold.

'What's B and B? Bed and Breakfast?'

'Hardly,' said Harold, his brow puckering with concentration.

'Betty and Someone Else beginning with B?' hazarded Frank.

Harold shook his head.

'If you were Irish,' went on Frank conversationally, 'I should suggest "Remember the Battle of the Boyne", but I suppose that's no help?'

'None,' said Harold. 'However, to get back to our muttons. You said Friday, June 23rd, I believe? Well, that's completely free, so count on me as a willing taxi-man.'

At that moment, Betty came in, bearing the tray with two steaming cups and a plate with gingernuts on it.

'Ah, Betty!' cried Harold. 'Put it here, my dear, and tell me something. Why have I got to remember "B and B" on June 22nd?'

'Coffee morning at the rectory,' said Betty promptly. 'Bring and Buy stall. You promised something to Mr Henstock when he came last week.'

Harold smiled his relief.

'I don't know what I'd do without you,' he told her, as she turned towards the door. 'Every home should have a Betty Bell.'

'Or a wife,' commented Frank. But Harold made no response, except to pass the coffee cup.

A day or two after this meeting, little Miss Fogerty paid another visit to the hospital.

Miss Watson was propped up on a bank of snowy pillows, surrounded by flowers and 'Get Well' cards. She was wearing a pale pink bed jacket, knitted by Agnes as a Christmas present a year or two earlier, that lady was pleased to see. That feather-and-shell pattern had been remarkably difficult to master, she remembered, but it certainly looked most attractive.

'It's so light and warm, Agnes dear,' said Dorothy, stroking the garment. 'And much admired by the nurses.'

Miss Fogerty grew pink with pleasure.

'I'm so glad. But, tell me, how are you getting on? And when will you be able to come home?'

'I *could* come out on Sunday next, but I think I shall stay a few days longer.'

She began to pleat the top of the sheet, and looked very near to tears, Agnes was horrified to see.

'You see, Ray came yesterday. Poor Kathleen was in bed with one of her migraine attacks.'

And very convenient those migraine attacks could be, thought Agnes tartly.

'So that she couldn't come, of course,' went on Dorothy. 'And it seems that they had arranged a holiday for the next two weeks, so that they can't have me there.'

'Come home,' urged Agnes. 'You know that I can help, and the district nurse would call daily. I'm sure we could manage.'

Miss Watson sniffed, and then blew her nose energetically.

'I do hope I'm not getting a cold,' she said, muffled in the handkerchief. Miss Fogerty was not deceived.

'You are the kindest soul on earth,' said Dorothy, recovering her composure. 'I've done quite a lot of thinking since Ray came, and if I stay here for another few days, gaining strength, I think I really will be able to manage at home. Perhaps someone could slip in at midday and get me a light lunch?'

Agnes thought at once of Nelly Piggott, but decided not to mention her just yet.

'If you would let me stay at the schoolhouse,' said Agnes diffidently, 'I could be with you at night, and bring you breakfast before going over to the school.'

'Oh, Agnes dear,' cried Miss Watson, the tears returning and now rolling down her cheeks unchecked. 'Oh, Agnes dear, *could* you? Would you mind? There's nothing I should like more.'

'I should love it,' said Agnes truthfully. 'We'll have a word with Sister and arrange a day next week.'

'And get the taxi from Lulling,' said Dorothy, already becoming more like her efficient, headmistress self. 'And we'll go back together. What a wonderful day it will be!'

She sighed happily, and wiped away the tears without subterfuge.

'It's only the relief, Agnes dear, and being so wobbly, you know. I can't begin to tell you how grateful I am to you, my dear. It's at times like this that one realises who one's true friends are.'

'Then that's settled,' said Agnes, 'and as soon as the doctor says you may leave, we'll go back to Thrush Green.'

'I can't wait! And now, Agnes dear, tell me how it's all going at school? Are the children behaving well? Is that wash-basin mended yet? Have those Cooke boys really got the mumps? Are there many forms from the office? How's the supply teacher managing? And has the piano-tuner been this term?'

Miss Fogerty was still answering questions when the nurse arrived to take Miss Watson's temperature.

'It's up a bit,' she commented as she shook the thermometer.

'I'm not surprised,' said her patient. 'It's excitement, of the nicest kind, that's done it.'

15 Early Summer

THE quiet mild weather which had ushered in June, now turned to a spell of gloriously hot sunshine.

Miss Fogerty looked out her sensible cotton frocks and Clark's sandals. Dotty Harmer spread sacks over the chicken run to provide her charges with extra shade. The rector took his lightweight clerical grey from the wardrobe, and Dimity hung it on the line to remove the faint smell of moth-balls. Winnie Bailey and Jenny erected the swing seat, and agreed that although the cretonne was shabby it 'would do another year'.

And, across the green, Nelly Piggott embarked on a mammoth washing spree, hauling down curtains, whisking off blankets and bedspreads, and even snatching up rugs from the floor to thrust into the soap suds.

Albert loathed it all, but recognising an irresistible force when he met it, resigned himself to the tornado of energy which whirled about him, and took advantage of the sunshine to do a little light tidying of the churchyard. Here, at least, there was peace.

He was engaged in picking a few weeds from the top of the stub wall which surrounded the graveyard when Dotty Harmer stopped to speak to him.

She was an arresting sight at the best of times, but today's summer outfit appeared to consist of a straight low-waisted frock, style circa 1920, made, it seemed, of deck-chair material, and ending just above the knees. A conical straw hat, like a coolie's, surmounted her thatch of grey hair, and lisle stockings, heavily wrinkled, led the eye down to a pair of grass-stained tennis shoes. She was accompanied by the faithful Flossie, now the picture of canine good health.

'I heard,' said Dotty, coming straight to the point, 'that your wife is looking for work. I wonder if she has heard that the Miss Lovelocks need temporary help?'

'Well, no, miss,' said Albert. He took off his greasy cap and scratched his lank hair. 'She ain't said nothin'. Maybe you'd like to tell her? She be washin'.'

'I can't stop now, I'm afraid. I have to meet the bus, at the bottom of the hill, but perhaps you would pass on the message?

'Very well, miss,' said Albert, unusually respectful. She might look a proper clown, but she was a lady for all that. Got a touch of her old Dad about her, that made you mind your manners, he thought.

He watched her figure receding into the distance, and turned back to the wall again. Yes, he'd tell Nelly when he went into dinner. Nice bit of cold fat bacon he had seen in the larder. A slice or two of that with pickled onions was something to relish, whatever the doctor said. It was a comforting thought.

The sun warmed his back as he pottered about his leisurley activities. He dwelt, with pleasure, upon the possibility of Nelly bringing in more money to the household. But best of all was the thought that he would be free of her company for a few hours. He only hoped that they would occur during opening time.

Edward Young had been busy with plans for converting the stable block into a roomy bungalow, and also for altering the top floor of their house into a self-contained flat.

The latter was a fairly straightforward job, for the attics had been divided into three good-sized bedrooms just before the 1914–1918 war. Old Mr Bassett remembered that his nurse had slept in one and, in those spacious days, the cook had had another, while two housemaids shared the third.

There was water already there, and the large dormer windows looked out upon splendid views. It could provide a lovely home for a single person, or perhaps a young couple. It was a conversion which Edward had had in mind for some time, and he submitted both plans together to the local planning committee.

The Bassetts preferred the stable block. For one thing, it was a ground floor abode, and for another, they were at a short distance from Joan and Edward, and both households could be independent, although close enough in an emergency to help each other.

Doctor Lovell's surmise that his patient would be stimulated by the plans now afoot, was fully justified. Robert took on a new lease of life, and pottered out to the stables with his foot-rule, planning where favourite pieces of furniture could be placed, how wide the windowsills could be, and other pleasurable activities. He now took a little exercise, or dozed in the sunny garden. His appetite improved and Milly and the family watched his return to health with the greatest satisfaction.

As soon as he was really fit, he and Milly proposed to return to Ealing to settle their affairs and to dispose of the business and the house.

Meanwhile, it was enough to enjoy the sunshine of Thrush Green, and to know that the future looked bright with hope.

Isobel Fletcher had replied with gratitude to the Hursts' letter, and said that she would not be free to accept their kind offer until early July, as prospective buyers seemed to be numerous, and there were several matters to arrange with her solicitor and the bank manager.

Williams and Frobisher had sent only one possibility, and it so happened that it was a house in which an old friend of her mother's had once lived. It had a long drive and far too much ground, and Isobel had turned it down as its upkeep would be too expensive. She hoped that she would have better luck while she was staying at Tullivers.

It was arranged that Winnie Bailey would keep the key, until Isobel was free to come, and that she would order milk, bread and groceries for her temporary next-door-neighbour.

Isobel rang Harold, as well as the Hursts, when she had made her decision.

'It was such a kind thing to think of,' said Isobel. 'What put it into your head?'

Harold could hardly say: 'The strongest desire to have you nearby,' but said that Frank had expressed some doubts about leaving the house empty, and knowing that she intended to return to her house-hunting, the two thoughts had gone together, and he hoped sincerely that it had not been a liberty.

'Far from it,' said Isobel warmly. 'I am terribly grateful to you, and I shall look forward to seeing you again before long.'

'And so shall I,' responded Harold, from the heart.

Nelly Piggott lost no time in calling upon the Misses Lovelock in Lulling High Street.

The sun was still warmly bathing Thrush Green in golden light when she set out from her home. It was half past six, and Albert was already next door at the Two Pheasants, despite Nelly's protestations.

From berating him, Nelly had turned to more womanly tactics, and on this particular evening, dressed in her finery for the forthcoming interview, and fragrant with attar of roses, she bestowed a rare kiss upon Albert's forehead.

'Just to please me, Albert dear,' she said, in her most seductive tones.

But Albert was not to be wooed.

'That soft soap,' he told her, shaking her off, 'don't cut any ice with me.'

With this splendid mixed metaphor as farewell, he then departed next door, leaving Nelly to collect her handbag and go off in the opposite direction.

She was not particularly upset by her failure to wean Albert from his beer. Nelly took a philosophical view of marriage. All men had their little weaknesses. If Albert's had not been liquor, it might have been wife-beating, or even infidelity, although Nelly was the first to admit that, with Albert's looks, a chance would be a fine thing.

She sailed down the hill and along Lulling High Street, relishing the evening sunshine and her own aura of attar of roses.

The three Misses Lovelock lived in a beautiful Georgian house halfway along the main street. Here they had been born, and the outside and the inside of their home had altered very little, except that there were far more *objets d'art* crowded inside than in their childhood days.

The Misses Lovelock were inveterate collectors, and rarely paid much for their pieces of porcelain, glass and silver. Older inhabitants of Lulling and Thrush Green knew this and were always on their guard when the sisters called.

Nelly pulled lustily at the old-fashioned iron bell pull at the side of the door, and Bertha opened it.

'I've come about the place, miss,' said Nelly politely.

Bertha's mind, somewhat bewildered, turned to fish. Had they ordered plaice? Perhaps Violet . . .

'I heard you was needing help in the house,' continued Nelly. 'But perhaps you're already suited?'

'Oh, *that* place!' exclaimed Bertha, light dawning. 'No, not yet. Do come in.'

She led the way into the dining-room which, despite the heat of the glorious day, struck cold and dark.

'If you'll sit down, Mrs Er?'

'Mrs Piggott,' said Nelly, sitting heavily on a delicate Sheraton chair. It creaked ominously, and Bertha felt some anxiety, not only for the chair's safety, but also at her visitor's identity. For, surely, this was the sexton's wife whose conduct had been so scandalous? Hadn't she run away with another man? Oh dear! What would Ada say?

'I will just go and tell my sisters that you are here. You do undertake housework, I suppose?'

'Yes'm. And cooking. I fairly loves cooking.'

'Yes, well—I won't be a moment.'

She fluttered off, leaving Nelly to cast a disparaging eye on the gloomy oil paintings, the heavy velvet curtains and the mammoth sideboard laden with half a hundredweight of assorted silverware. The work the gentry made for themselves!

Bertha, breaking in upon Ada's crochet work and Violet's tussle with *The Times* crossword puzzle, gave a breathless account of their visitor.

Her two sisters lowered their work slowly, and surveyed her with disapproval.

'But why invite such a person into the house?' asked Ada.

'But can she undertake housework?' asked Violet, more practically.

'Because I didn't know who she was,' cried Bertha, answering Ada, 'and she can certainly do housework. I remember Winnie Bailey telling me what a marvellous job she made of Thrush Green School,' she went on, turning to Violet.

The three sisters exchanged glances of doubt and indecision.

'And another thing,' continued Bertha, 'I've just remembered that she is a first-class cook. It was Winnie who told me that too.'

Ada sighed.

'Well, I suppose we'd better see this person now that she's here.'

She rolled up her crochet work in an exquisite silk scarf, and put it on one side. Violet placed *The Times* on the sofa.

Together the three sisters advanced upon the dining-room. Nelly struggled to her feet as they entered, the chair creaking with relief.

'Do sit down,' said Ada graciously. The three sisters took seats on the other side of the table, and Nelly lowered herself again into the long-suffering chair, and faced them.

'Let me tell you what we require,' said Ada. 'Our present helper is looking after her daughter who is just about to be confined. She will probably be home again in six weeks or so.'

'Yes'm,' said Nelly, surveying the three wrinkled faces before her. Never seen three such scarecrows all together before, she was thinking. Why, they couldn't weigh twenty stone between 'em!

'Two mornings a week, one of them a Friday, but any other morning which would be convenient for you would be quite in order with us.'

She glanced at her sisters who nodded in agreement.

'Tuesday would suit me best,' said Nelly, thinking of washing day on Monday.

'And I hear that you are an excellent cook, Mrs Piggott.'

Nelly smiled in acknowledgement.

'Perhaps, very occasionally, you might prepare luncheon for us?'

'I'd be pleased to,' said Nelly. She waited to hear about payment.

'Have you brought any references?' enquired Ada.

'Well, no,' confessed Nelly. 'But Miss Watson would speak for me, and the Allens at the Drover's Arms.

There was a whispered consultation between the three sisters, and much nodding of trembling heads.

'Very well,' said Ada. 'As this will only be a temporary arrangement we will waive the references. When can you start?'

Nelly decided that she must take a firm stand.

'I should like to know the wages, ma'am, before saying "Yes" or "No".'

'We pay fifty pence an hour, Mrs Piggott, and should like three hours each morning. You would receive three pounds a week.'

Fifty pence! thought Nelly. It was the least she had ever been offered, but it would be useful, and the job looked like being one after her own heart.

Ada, seeing the hesitation, added swiftly: 'You would be paid extra, of course, if you prepared a meal while you were here. Another fifty pence, Violet? Bertha?'

'Oh, yes, indeed,' they quavered obediently.

Nelly rose.

'Then I'll come next Tuesday,' she said. 'Nine o'clock?'

'I think nine-thirty,' said Ada. 'We breakfast a little late, now that we are approaching middle age.'

She rose too, and the three sisters ushered Nelly out of the front door into Lulling High Street.

'Approaching middle age,' repeated Nelly to herself, as she set off for Thrush Green. 'That's a laugh! They must be over eighty, every one of them! Well, I shan't make a fortune there, but it'll be a nice change from cleaning Albert's place.'

It was on one of these cloudless June days that the Hursts flew to America.

Harold, as promised, drove them to Heathrow airport. The sun was hot through the glass and all were in high spirits. Neither Frank nor his wife were anxious travellers, Harold was glad to see. Much travelled himself, he had always felt slightly irritated by his fellow companions who were constantly leafing through their wallets to check that they had passports, licences, tickets and all the other paraphernalia of travelling, or turning to each other with agitated queries, such as: 'Did you turn off the electricity? The water? Did we leave a key with Florrie? Did you remember to tell the police we would be away? Do you think Rover will *like* those new kennels?'

Frank seemed to have everything in hand, and was looking forward to visiting the United States again, and to introducing Phil to his friends there. He loved the warmth and generosity of American hospitality, and the enthusiasm of his audiences. It made one feel young again. He hoped that Jeremy would pay many visits there as he grew older.

That young man was full of excited chatter. Harold let the boy's commentary on the passing scene flow in one ear and out at the other. He was remembering another trip he had taken to Heathrow, with Phil, some years before.

Then she had sat, white and silent, beside him, for the news had just come through of her first husband's death in a car crash in France, and Harold had driven her straight to the airport.

How bleak the outlook had seemed then! Harold's heart had been sore for her, so young and defenceless, with the added responsibility of bringing up a young child on her own. Thank God she had met Frank, and this second marriage had turned out so well.

His mind turned to Charles again and his happy marriage. And then, naturally enough, to the pleasant thought of Isobel coming to stay at Tullivers before long. Would the future hold marriage for him, he wondered?

He turned into the lane leading to the airport.

'Here we are! Here we are!' carolled Jeremy. 'And there are thousands of planes! Look, look! Don't you wish you were coming too, Uncle Harold?'

'In some ways,' replied Harold circumspectly, 'but I think I'd just as soon stay at Thrush Green for a while.'

16 Problems for the Piggotts

MISS WATSON came home from hospital on a Saturday, which meant that Agnes Fogerty could collect her in the taxi, as arranged, and see her settled at the schoolhouse.

Apart from looking pale and rather shaken, Dorothy Watson had come through her ordeal very well. She leant heavily on two sticks, but managed to get into the taxi without much trouble, and was in fine spirits.

'To be out again, Agnes dear,' she cried. 'To feel fresh air on one's face, and to see children *running*! I can't tell you how lovely it is!'

Agnes had put some early roses in Dorothy's bedroom, and everything that could be done by loving hands awaited the invalid. The bed was turned down, a hot bottle was swathed in a fresh nightgown, and that day's newspaper and letters awaited reading on the bedside table.

Miss Watson, who had been looking forward to having lunch downstairs, saw that she must give way graciously to Agnes's ministrations. Nevertheless, she insisted on limping round downstairs, admiring the care which had been lavished on all her possessions.

'And Betty Bell has made you a sponge cake,' said Agnes. 'It's from Mr Shoosmith, with his love.'

'His love?' echoed Dorothy. 'How kind! He's such a reserved man, I should have been more than gratified with "kind regards". A sponge cake, and *love* as well, really touches me.'

'He's a very thoughtful person,' said Agnes. 'Yesterday he sent Piggott round to tidy the garden here instead of his own, and he has enquired many times about you.'

Miss Watson made her way slowly to the kitchen window at the rear of the house, and gazed with pleasure at the garden. Her roses were beginning to break, and the violas edging the beds were gay with blue, white and yellow blooms. A harassed blackbird, followed by four babies larger than itself, scurried to and fro across the newly-mown lawn, snatching up any morsel available and returning to thrust it down the clamorous throats.

She opened the window and leant across the sill. All the scents of summer drifted in upon the warm air, the mingled potpourri of the jasmine on the wall, the old-fashioned crimson peonies nearby, the freshly-cut grass, and the hay field beyond which stretched to the distant greenery of Lulling Woods.

There, in the distance, was Dotty Harmer's cottage, sitting as snugly as a golden cat in the fold of the meadow. Near at hand, glowing just as effulgently in the sunshine, was the bulk of kind Harold Shoosmith's home, and her own beloved little school.

She drew in her breath, overcome by the bliss of being at Thrush Green again, and suddenly realised how tired she was.

She turned to Agnes.

'Wonderful to be back, my dear. And now I'm going to that lovely bed, if you will help me with my shoes and stockings.'

She mounted the stairs slowly, attended anxiously by little Miss Fogerty, and as soon as she entered the bedroom went to gaze upon Thrush Green from the front windows.

There were the chestnut trees in pride of leaf. There were the homes of her friends and neighbours, sturdy, warm and welcoming. Nathaniel Patten gleamed upon his plinth, and gazed benevolently upon the children playing on the swings and see-saw nearby. A pale blue cloudless sky arched over all, and somewhere, close at hand, a blackbird trilled.

Miss Watson turned back into the room.

'What a perfect day, in all ways!' she commented. 'But, best of all, Agnes, to have you here with me. I am a very lucky woman!'

*   *   *

One sunny afternoon, soon after Miss Watson's return to her home, although not yet to her school duties, she noticed a familiar figure entering the gate of the Youngs' house.

'Now what can Molly Piggott—I mean Molly Curdle—be doing in Thrush Green?' she wondered. She had always been fond of the girl. She had been a rewarding pupil, keen to learn and polite in manner, despite her deplorable old father.

Miss Watson had watched her progress as mother's help at the Youngs', with the greatest interest and approval, and her marriage to young Ben Curdle had won everyone's blessing at Thrush Green.

Joan Young was as surprised to see Molly as Miss Watson had been, but welcomed her warmly.

She led her visitor into the garden and they sat in the shade of the ancient apple tree which Molly knew so well. Young Paul's swing had hung there, and she had spent many hours pushing her charge to and fro beneath spring blossom, summer leaf, and autumn fruit.

In the heat of the day the dappled shade was welcome, and Molly pushed her damp hair from her forehead.

'That hill gets steeper,' she smiled. 'Or I'm getting older.'

Her eyes roamed to the stable block. Preliminary clearing had begun, in the hope of planning permission being granted, and a stack of assorted and cumbersome objects, ranging from derelict deck-chairs to an equally decrepit cupboard, leant against the wall.

'That's a heavy job,' commented Molly. 'You planning to use the place as a garage?'

'Not a garage,' said Joan. 'Something more ambitious than that.'

She told the girl about her parents' retirement, and the conversions that they hoped to make. Molly nodded enthusiastically.

'I'm glad they're coming back at last to Thrush Green,' she said. 'It's only right that Mr Bassett should be here. Are they here now?'

'At the moment they are at the Henstocks having tea. Which reminds me, Molly, I've offered you nothing—which is shameful. What can I get you?'

'Nothing, thank you. Well, perhaps a glass of water?'

'I'll bring you some home-made lemonade. The same recipe you used to make up when you were here, remember?'

'Indeed I do. I'll come and help.'

They went back into the cool kitchen to fetch their drinks, and Joan wondered what had brought the girl to Thrush Green.

As if guessing her thoughts, Molly spoke.

'Friends of ours had a bit of business to do today over here, and offered me a lift. Ben's minding George, so I thought I'd look in and see Dad, and you, and anybody else as remembered me.'

'We all remember you,' cried Joan, leading the way with the tray, back to the garden seat.

They sipped their lemonade, the ice clinking against the glass. Above them a starling chattered, his dark plumage iridescent in the sunlight. A fat thrush ran about the lawn, stopping every now and again, head cocked sideways, to listen for a worm beneath the surface.

'I wondered,' said Molly, breaking the silence, 'if you'd heard of anything for Ben to do?'

Joan felt a pang of guilt. She had certainly made enquiries, and mentioned the matter to several friends, but the advent of her parents, and the anxiety over her father's health had limited her search.

'I haven't done as much as I had hoped to do,' she confessed. She outlined her efforts, and promised to make amends.

'The thing is,' said Molly, 'Dick Hasler has offered us a good sum for the fair, and Ben thinks he'll have to accept. There's no end of expense that we can't face. I left him patching up two swingboats. The timber alone cost a mint of money, and there's a limit to the time Ben can spare for repairs. We've faced it now. We'll have to give up, and although it grieves my Ben, we know the fair's day's done—at least, as we ran it. Dick's got plenty behind him, and if he loses on one thing he can make it up on another.'

'In fact, what he loses on the swings, he gains on the roundabouts?' smiled Joan.

'That's it exactly. And this is where we'd like to be for the future, as you know.'

'You're quite right. There's your father to consider too, although I expect you know that Nelly's back?'

'Yes, indeed. One look at that place showed me that. I can't say I take to Nelly,' she went on, in a burst of confidence. 'She's too bold for my liking, but she do keep a house clean.'

'And keeps Albert well fed.'

'But for how long? D'you think she'll stay? In some ways, I hope she will. It would be a relief to us to know Dad was being looked after. But they're not happy together, as you know. I can't see it lasting.'

'Frankly, neither can I,' agreed Joan.

St Andrew's church clock chimed four, and Molly put down her glass hastily.

'I'd best be getting down to the crossroads. I'm being picked up at a quarter past, and I must drop into Dad's again to say goodbye.'

'Now, I promise to do my best to find something for Ben,' said Joan, taking the girl's hands in hers. 'When would he be free to start?'

'Any time,' said Molly. 'We could stay with Dad until we found a place of our own. Anything to get back to Thrush Green, and to start afresh. It's been a sad time for us lately, particularly for Ben. The fair's always been his life, as you know.'

'Something will turn up, I'm positive,' Joan assured her. 'I will write to you very soon.'

She watched Molly cross the grass to go to Albert's cottage. The children were streaming out from school, and Joan thought how lovely it would be when Molly and Ben were back, and George himself would be coming home from Thrush Green School.

Nelly Piggott missed seeing Molly by a mere half hour, as Albert pointed out.

Nelly had been shopping after her bout of housework, and her first attempt to cook lunch for the three sisters.

She was hot, tired and cross. Her corsets were too tight, and so were her shoes. She took scant notice of Albert's remarks, as she filled the kettle at the sink, and Albert resented it.

'I said that our Molly'd called,' he repeated loudly.

'*Your* Molly, not ours,' replied Nelly. 'She's nothing to me.'

'No need to be so white and spiteful,' grumbled Albert. 'Specially as she said how nice the place looked.'

'No thanks to her,' rejoined Nelly, struggling to take off her shoes. 'Fat lot she does for her old Dad, I must say.'

'They sends me money, don't they?' demanded Albert. 'Regular.'

'And where does that go? Down your throat, the bulk of it. I tell you straight, Albert, I shan't be stopping here long if you don't give me more housekeeping.'

'Well, you've left here before, and I shan't stop you clearing off again. When you gets into these tantrums I'd sooner see the back of you, and that's that!'

Nelly reached for the teapot. Things were going a little too fast for her.

'Want a cup?' she asked, more gently.

'May as well.'

'Don't strain yourself,' said Nelly tartly, spooning tea into the pot. She set out cups upon a tray, and poured the tea. They sipped in silence.

Albert was weighing up the pros and cons of life with Nelly, an exercise which he undertook frequently.

Nelly was reviewing the situation which she had taken on at the Lovelocks'. Could she, she asked herself, continue for six whole weeks, albeit only twice a week, in the present frustrating circumstances?

It was the *meanness* of the three ladies which infuriated Nelly. It was one thing to find that the dusters provided consisted of squares cut from much-worn undergarments, but quite another to be denied the tin of furniture polish.

Miss Violet had undone the lid, selected one of the deplorable squares, and scooped out about a teaspoonful of the polish upon it.

'That,' she told Nelly, 'should be *quite* enough for the dining-room.'

Seeing Nelly's amazed countenance, she had added swiftly: 'Come to me again, Nelly, if you need more, although I hardly think you will find it necessary.'

She had swept from the room, tin in hand, leaving Nelly speechless.

All the cleaning equipment was handed out in the same parsimonious style. A small puddle of Brasso in a cracked saucer was supposed to cope with the many brass objects in the house. Vim was handled as though it were gold-dust. Washing-up liquid was measured by the thimbleful. It was more than Nelly could stand, and she said so.

Her complaints brought very little improvement, and Nelly retaliated by cleaning all that she could, and leaving the rest as soon as the rations for the day ran out. But she resented it bitterly. She *liked* to see things clean, and never stinted cleaning agents in her own home.

However, she comforted herself with the thought that it was only for six weeks, maybe less. Surely, she could stick it out for that time, especially as nothing else had cropped up to give her alternative employment?

The memory of the lunch she had been obliged to cook made her shudder. Nelly respected food, and always chose the best when shopping. It was no good being a first-class cook, as she knew she was, if the materials were poor. You might just as well try to paint a portrait with creosote.

When Miss Bertha had fluttered into the kitchen that morning, and had asked her to cook that day's luncheon,

Nelly's spirits had risen. She had visions of rolling out the lightest of pastry, of whipping eggs and cream, of tenderising steak or skinning some delicate fish cooked in butter.

'And you will stay to have some too, Nelly, I hope.'

'Thank you, ma'am,' said Nelly, envisaging herself at the kitchen table with a heaped plate of her own excellent cooking. Albert had been left with a cold pork-pie, some home-made brawn, strong cheese and pickled shallots, so Nelly had no qualms on his behalf. She had told him that she intended to shop in the afternoon. Really, things had worked out very well, she told herself, and this would save her going to the Fuchsia Bush for a cup of coffee and a sandwich, as she had planned.

Miss Bertha vanished into the larder and appeared with a small piece of smoked fillet of cod. It was the tail end, very thin, and weighed about six ounces. To Nelly's experienced eye it might provide one rather inferior helping, if eked out with, say, a poached egg on top.

'Well, here we are,' said Bertha happily. 'If you could poach this and share it between three, I mean, *four*, of course.'

'Is this all?' enquired Nelly flabbergasted. 'Why, our cat would polish that off and look for more!'

Miss Bertha appeared not to hear, as she made her way back to the larder, leaving Nelly gazing at the fish with dismay.

'You'd like poached eggs with this, I take it?' said Nelly.

Bertha put two small eggs carefully beside the fish.

'We prefer scrambled eggs, Nelly. These two, well beaten, should be ample for us all.'

'There won't be enough,' said Nelly flatly.

'We add a little milk.'

'Horrible!' protested Nelly. 'Should never be done with scrambled eggs. Butter's all you need, and a little pepper and salt.'

'Not *butter*!' gasped Bertha. 'We always use margarine in cooking. *Butter* would be *most* extravagant!'

Nelly began to see that she would certainly need to visit the Fuchsia Bush to supplement the starvation diet being planned.

'Vegetables?' she managed to ask.

'Plenty of spinach, Nelly, in the garden, and I thought some rhubarb for pudding. There is still some growing by the cold frame. I will leave out the sugar for you.'

'Very well, ma'am,' she said as politely as her outraged sensibilities would allow.

She finished drying the breakfast things, and went, basket in hand to fetch the spinach and rhubarb. On her return, she found half a cupful of granulated sugar awaiting its union with the rhubarb, and about half an ounce of margarine.

Nelly left the spinach to soak, and wiped the thin sticks of rhubarb. They were well past their best, and showed rusty marks when she chopped them.

For the rest of the morning Nelly seethed over the appalling ingredients which were to make a lunch for four people.

'Not enough for a sparrow,' she muttered to herself, as she went about her chores. 'And all windy stuff too. If those old scarecrows is doubled up this afternoon, it won't be my fault, and that's flat!'

She cooked the food as best she could. It grieved her to be using margarine instead of butter, but there was nothing else to use, and mighty little of that.

Miss Violet had set the table. The heavy Georgian silver gleamed, the glasses sparkled, and handmade lace mats lay like snowflakes on the polished mahogany.

Nelly carried in the dish of fish and scrambled egg and placed it before Miss Ada at the head of the table. Her face expressed scorn.

'I took the liberty, ma'am,' said Nelly, 'of picking a sprig of parsley to garnish it.'

Miss Ada inclined her head graciously.

'You did quite rightly,' she said. 'It all looks delicious.'

Nelly returned to the kitchen and surveyed the teaspoonful of food upon her plate. At that moment, the cat leapt through the window.

'Here,' said Nelly, handing down the plate, 'try your luck with that.'

Delicately, with infinite caution, the cat sniffed at the food. A rose petal tongue emerged to lick the fish tentatively, then the cat shuddered slightly, and turned away.

'And I don't blame you,' said Nelly. She threw the scraps out of the window, and watched a gaggle of sparrows descend upon them.

'What I could do to a nice fillet steak!' mourned Nelly, preparing to carry in the dish of sour rhubarb, unadorned by any such rich accompaniment as cream or custard.

Later, when Nelly had washed up and had been complimented upon her cooking by the three old ladies, Nelly tried to forget the whole shocking experience. Never again, she told herself, never again! Not if they went down on their brittle old bended knees would she be party to such a travesty of cooking! It was more than flesh and blood could stand.

It was hardly surprising that Albert found her exceptionally snappy that evening. Nelly had suffered much.

Part Three

Safe Arrival

17 Living Alone

MISS WATSON's enforced rest gave her plenty of time to think. Not that she did not think in her normal state, but this was thinking at a different level.

She was a healthy busy woman, who ran her school and her home with competence. Her mind was always occupied with such diverse matters as ordering fresh stock, arranging a parents' evening, supervising the new probationer-teacher, as well as remembering to order an extra pint of milk because the Henstocks were coming to coffee, to send the spare-room bedspread to the laundry, and to ring the hairdresser to see if she could fit in a permanent wave on a Saturday morning.

These day to day activities left little time for such things as general reading, although she conscientiously tried to keep abreast with present-day writings on education. She rarely visited the theatre in term time, and her travels had been limited to less expensive areas in Europe. She kept up with a few old friends, and saw Ray and Kathleen several times a year, but this was the first occasion when she had been thrown upon her own resources and had experienced solitude, without activity, for hours at a time.

In this present vague post-operation daze, she found reading irksome, and radio and television equally tiring. She was content to lie back and let her mind dwell upon a great many aspects of life which, until now, she had largely ignored.

It was something of a shock to realise that one was not completely self supporting. So far in her life, she had managed her affairs without needing to ask for any help, other than such specialised aid necessary for coping with tax affairs and other money matters, or the occasional legal problem which dear old Justin Venables in Lulling managed with easy experience.

She had never before suffered such physical weakness as now engulfed her, and it was unnerving to find that she needed help to cope with such everyday matters as bathing, dressing and moving about the house. She felt confident that she would be back to normal in a few weeks, but then how could one be sure that other similar accidents might not occur, as one grew older? It was a sobering thought. If the present mishap had occurred when the school had closed, and she had been alone, how long, she wondered, could she have lain there unattended?

Thank heaven for dear Agnes! It would have been impossible to return to her own home without Agnes's help. She dwelt now upon the sterling qualities of her staunch assistant. Her presence in the house, particularly at night, when she felt at her most vulnerable, was wonderfully consoling, and although she had been careful not to disturb Agnes's much needed slumber, it was a great comfort to know that she was there if the emergency arose.

Soon, of course, she must face the fact that Agnes would return to Mrs White's. But need she?

Miss Watson toyed with the idea of inviting dear Agnes

to share her home permanently. It would be to their mutual advantage, she felt sure. The only thing was the uncomfortable fact that Agnes might not want to give up the independence she so much enjoyed.

Miss Watson turned over the problem in her mind, with unusual humility. What right had she to expect Agnes to want to live with her? She had been more than fortunate to find a friend so unselfish that she was prepared to look after her for these few weeks. It was asking too much of her to expect that she would want to remain.

And yet Agnes would be the perfect companion! She grew fonder of her as the years passed. She was a fine person, loyal and kind, much more noble, in every way, than her headmistress, thought Dorothy sadly.

No, it would not be fair to ask her, she decided, with a sigh. Agnes might well agree simply because she felt that she was needed to help, ignoring her own feelings.

She was so unselfish. It was very uplifting to live with a saint, but it had its problems.

Next door, Harold Shoosmith was also in a state of turmoil. Isobel would soon be arriving, and he hoped that he would be able to greet her without showing the real depths of his feelings. It was quite alarming to find how often his thoughts turned to her, and he was beginning to fear that the observant residents of Thrush Green might guess the cause of his preoccupation.

He was about to cross the green one morning, to mow the grass at Tullivers, when Dotty Harmer appeared, looking even more agitated than usual.

'You haven't seen Flossie, by any chance?' she called, hastening towards him.

'Flossie?' queried Harold.

'My dog. My little spaniel. She's run off, you see.'

'No, I'm sorry. I will keep an eye open for her.'

'It's so upsetting,' continued Dotty, hitching up a stocking with a claw-like hand. 'I fear she must be on heat, and I hadn't realised it.'

She peered at Harold sharply.

'I don't embarrass you, I trust?'

'Not in the least,' responded Harold. 'I have been aware of the facts of life for some years now.'

Any gentle sarcasm intended was lost upon Dotty, in her present state of perturbation.

'Of course, of course! But it is so annoying. She may have gone along to Nidden. There is a collie dog there, at the farm, to whom she is rather partial. The results of such a liaison would not be acceptable to the Kennel Club, I fear, but there it is.'

'Well, I'll certainly keep a look out, but it might be as well to call at the rector's, or Miss Bembridge's. They might catch her before she gets into the traffic at Lulling. Would you care to use my telephone?'

'You are most kind! Most kind! But I think I will walk across while I'm here. Besides, I am disturbing your activities.'

'I was only going to cut the grass at Tullivers,' said Harold.

Dotty's wrinkled countenance lit up with pleasure.

'All ready for Isobel? She will be grateful, I'm sure.'

She fluttered off in the direction of Ella's house, leaving Harold to his thoughts.

*   *   *

Betty Bell, always exuberant, seemed to bring Isobel Fletcher's name into the conversation more frequently than Harold could have wished, but he had the sense to hold his tongue on these occasions. There was no point in adding fuel to the fire, he told himself.

But, one morning, Betty arrived in a rare state of indignation.

'D'you know what?' she demanded. 'That fat Nelly Piggott's been trying to get my job off of me!'

'What, here?' asked Harold, alarmed.

'No, no! I'd see you was looked after,' said Betty, as though indulging a backward child. 'No need for you to worry. No, that besom—excuse my French—has been crawling round Miss Fogerty, I hear, and would have gone in to see Miss Watson too, if Miss Fogerty hadn't put her foot down. The very idea!'

'She wasn't successful, I take it,' ventured Harold.

'I should hope not!' snorted Betty. 'Why, I keeps that place *beautiful*! *Beautiful*, I tell you! Toffee papers, squashed chalk, bubble gum and all. You could eat your dinner off of the floor when I've done with it.'

'I'm sure you could,' Harold agreed, wondering why anyone should be expected to want to eat dinners from floors or, for that matter, why it should occur to anyone to *serve* dinners in such a peculiarly uncomfortable position.

'And if I sees her about,' went on Betty wrathfully, 'I shall give her a piece of my mind!'

'I shouldn't bother,' said Harold, alarmed at the prospect of a noisy row on Thrush Green.

'Or the flat of my hand,' added Betty, and flung out of the room.

*　　*　　*

There was sudden activity at the Youngs' house. Edward's plans had been passed with unusual rapidity, and the builders, whom he had alerted earlier, were beginning to move in with all their paraphernalia.

Milly and Robert decided that they would make their way back to Ealing.

'I've no excuse for lingering,' said Mr Bassett. 'Thrush Green has put me on my feet again, and we shall only be in your way with the building going on. It's time we went back and put our affairs in order.'

'We shall miss you,' said Joan, 'but you'll be back for good before long. What a marvellous thought!'

'For us too,' said Milly. 'We've been blessed with two wonderful daughters. This would have been a terrible time for us without you to help.'

A week later, Edward drove them to Ealing in their own car, with Joan following behind. They settled the parents in the house, and were relieved to find that Frank had taken an hour or two off work to welcome them home, and to give Robert the latest news of the business.

'I shall be relieved to have them near us,' said Joan, as they drove back to Thrush Green together. 'How long do you think it will be before the stable block is ready?'

'Quicker than builders usually are!' promised Edward. 'I'll see to that!'

It was mid-July before Isobel was freed from her affairs in Sussex.

She arrived on a sunny afternoon, and spent an hour with her new next-door neighbour, Winnie Bailey, before unlocking the door of Tullivers.

Isobel looked tired, Winnie thought, as she poured tea for them both, but then she had had a long journey and probably a good deal of worry in the last few weeks.

'No, still nothing definitely settled,' said Isobel, in reply to her query. 'You know how it is with selling a house. If my present would-be buyers can sell their own, all's well. But they're waiting to see if *their* buyer can sell *his*. How far back the queue stretches, heaven alone knows.'

'And it only needs one to default, I suppose, for the whole chain to collapse?'

'Exactly. Never mind, here I am, and Williams and Frobisher have sent me four possibilities, so I shall go ahead and enjoy looking at them. Better still, it's lovely to think I have so much more time to spend in Thrush Green. Tell me how everyone is.'

Winnie told her about the Youngs' plans.

'Lucky Bassetts! I envy them the stable conversion. If I didn't want a small house and garden, I think I'd rush across and plead for the top floor flat! Someone's going to have a nice home there.'

Winnie went on to tell her about Ben and Molly Curdle, the Henstocks, Ella, and finally, Harold.

'He's worked so hard in the garden,' said Winnie. 'The lawn looks immaculate, and the roses at Tullivers are the best at Thrush Green.'

'Let's go and see it,' cried Isobel jumping up. 'I feel a new woman after that tea. Once I've unpacked, I shall go to see Harold. He must have been working so hard.'

'I'm sure it was a labour of love,' said Winnie.

But Isobel, leading the way, did not appear to hear.

Now that Isobel had arrived, Harold's happiness grew daily, but he was anxious not to call too frequently at Tullivers, and so lay open the unsuspecting Isobel to the wagging tongues of Thrush Green.

Isobel, as it happened, was not so unsuspecting as Harold imagined. She was used to the admiration of men, and liked their company. An exceptionally happy marriage and a wide circle of friends had given her ease of manner with the opposite sex, and Harold's feelings, although carefully concealed, were guessed by the sympathetic Isobel.

In such a small community it was inevitable that they saw each other frequently, and they enjoyed each other's company more and more.

Isobel took Harold to see some of the places which she had

known well in her girlhood around Stow, north of Thrush Green, and he accompanied her to look at one or two of the houses which Williams and Frobisher had recommended.

On the whole, it was a dispiriting job. The houses which were large enough to house the furniture which Isobel wanted to keep, were usually much too large, with endless corridors, high ceilings, and a formidable number of stairs. Those which were of manageable proportions were sometimes thatched, which Isobel disliked, or the rooms were small and stuffy.

'What I want is something in between,' sighed Isobel, as they emerged from one such cottage, Harold almost bent double to miss striking his head on the porch. 'I'm beginning to wonder if I shall ever find what I want.'

'Cheer up,' said Harold. 'I went through all this too when I was looking. It's disheartening for you, but I must confess I'm thoroughly enjoying myself.'

Isobel laughed. 'Well, I should have given up long ago if you hadn't been such a support. It's made all the difference to have some company.'

Harold seemed about to speak, thought better of it, and opened the door of the Alfa Romeo for her.

'Are you feeling strong enough to face "a bijou residence set like a gem amidst panoramic views"?' asked Isobel, consulting her papers.

'I can face any amount of them,' replied Harold bravely.

'Right,' said Isobel, letting in the clutch. 'It's about three miles from here.'

'And after that,' said Harold, 'I'm taking you to lunch at the Fleece. You need to keep up your strength when house-hunting.'

*   *   *

Little Miss Fogerty was as delighted as Harold to have Isobel at Thrush Green, and visited Tullivers frequently.

Miss Watson was now back at school, limping about her duties with a stick, and thankful to be of some use again. Agnes was very anxious about her, and insisted that she returned to her bed for a rest after school dinner and this Miss Watson agreed to do, with surprising meekness.

Now that she was back, the supply teacher departed, much to the relief of all.

'I'm quite sure she did her best,' Agnes told Dorothy earnestly. 'She was very *sincere* and *conscientious*, and most diligent in reading reports, and the leaders in *The Times Educational Supplement*, but I think she found the children rather a nuisance.'

'A case of putting the cart before the horse,' agreed Dorothy. 'It's good to be back on our own.'

It also meant that Agnes had more time to see Isobel, and the two old friends had much to talk about. It was clear to Isobel that Agnes still worried about Miss Watson being alone in the house.

'She's still very unsteady,' she told Isobel. 'One stumble, and she'd be quite helpless, you know.'

'You must let her do as she wishes,' comforted Isobel. 'After all, it could happen anyway, whether you were in the house or not. I'm sure she will be sensible. Lots of women have to live alone. Look at me!'

'But do you *like* living alone? I mean, I'm quite glad to know that the Whites are under the same roof as I am when I go up to bed. It makes me feel safer.'

'No, I can't say that I like living alone,' said Isobel

thoughtfully. 'But then I'm not used to it yet.'

'Perhaps,' ventured Agnes, 'you might, in time, of course, marry again.'

'I can't imagine it,' said Isobel. 'At our age, Agnes dear, one doesn't think about it. No, I think I shall be quite happy if I can find a little house here, and know that I'm safely among friends. One really can't ask for more.'

The hot weather continued, one blazing day following the other. Harold Shoosmith reverted to his practice of taking a siesta, as he had throughout his working life overseas, and most of Thrush Green did the same.

The nights seemed to be as hot as the days, and when the full moon shone through Harold's window, he flung off the sheet which was his only covering, and wandered about the house.

A field of corn stretched towards Nidden, and ran hard by his boundary hedge. He leant from the window, relishing a faint breeze that ruffled his hair refreshingly.

In the moonlight the corn was silvered, glowing with an unearthly sheen. In the heat of the day, he had heard the ripe ears crackling under the fierce sun. The harvest would be early this year, although the farmers were already predicting a light yield. What would be in the field next, he wondered? And would Isobel be here by then to see it?

An owl's cry trembled upon the air, and soon he saw the bird swoop silently from a lone oak, sailing downwind upon its rounded wings. What a vast number of lovely things one could see at night, normally missed by having one's head on the pillow! A restless night had its compensations, he decided.

He crossed the landing, and went to see Thrush Green from the window of the front bedroom. The moonlight was so bright that he could see all the houses clearly. It gleamed upon Nathaniel Patten's bald bronze pate, and edged the folds of his frock-coat with silver. A cat was sitting on the plinth at his feet, washing its face.

Harold's eye travelled from Ella's cottage on his far right across the grass, along to Winnie Bailey's, and then next door to Tullivers where, he hoped, Isobel was having a less wakeful night. She had been to see yet another house that afternoon, although on this occasion she had gone alone.

Harold felt deeply sorry for her in this fruitless search, and his mind turned, once again, to the problem that concerned him. How much simpler it would be if she would marry him and live here! But would she want to? And could he ask her, so soon after her husband's death?

He had no doubts now about his own feelings. More than anything in the world he wanted to marry Isobel, and he could think of nothing else.

Harold sighed, and returned to his restless pacing about the house. He knew his own feelings well enough, but what were Isobel's?

18 Hope for the Curdles

JOAN YOUNG, mindful of her promise to Molly about looking out for an opening for Ben, now set about the task with extra zeal.

With her parents back in Ealing, she had more time to devote to her own affairs. She heard of several jobs, but somehow none seemed quite right for Ben. She was beginning to despair, and told Edward so.

'I'm seeing Tim Collet this afternoon,' he said. 'I'll have a word with him.'

Collets was a family firm of agricultural engineers in Lulling. It had been in existence for over a hundred years. Originally a blacksmith's, such simple tools as scythes, bill-hooks, horse ploughs and pig troughs figured largely in the early years of the firm. More sophisticated equipment such as threshing machines and harvesters soon came along, giving way eventually to the complicated monsters, costing thousands of pounds, which modern farming demanded.

The business was now run by two Collet brothers, Tim and Bob. They were shrewd and hard-working, and employed a dozen or so skilled men. It was the sort of work which Ben would enjoy and would be capable of carrying out. Joan only hoped that there might be a vacancy.

Luck was with them. Tim Collet told Edward that the man

in charge of the yard was leaving at Michaelmas, and he was promoting another elderly employee to take his place, so that there would be a job available.

'I was going to advertise it,' said Tim, 'but if young Curdle wants to apply tell him to come and see me as soon as possible. I knew the old lady pretty well, and Ben too. You could trust him anywhere, which is more than you can say for some of 'em these days.'

When Edward told Joan this news, she broached another subject which had been in her mind for some days.

'Edward,' she began, 'if Ben gets this job —'

'Could they have the top flat?' finished Edward for her, and then laughed.

'You're too clever by half,' said Joan.

'Not really. I thought of it when I was talking to Tim. It would be a great help to us if Molly were here to give you a hand. There's bound to be more to do when the parents live here, and I'm sure she would want to have a little job too.'

'I'll write tonight and tell them the position. We certainly couldn't have better tenants,' agreed Joan. 'But will the flat be ready by September?'

'Pretty well, I think. If not, we can put them up, I'm sure. Unless Ben insists on sleeping at Albert's, of course!'

'Poor Ben! We'll make sure that doesn't have to happen. And in any case, I expect Nelly's in the spare bed.'

'She'd be a fool if she wasn't,' said Edward.

As it happened, at that moment Nelly was a long way from the spare bed, but busy in the Misses Lovelocks' kitchen washing up greasy plates.

The end of her six weeks' sojourn was in sight, and Nelly had heard, with considerable relief, that the usual help was returning to her duties before long.

She had sworn privately never to cook another meal in that house. However, she had been prevailed upon to cook 'a nice little piece of lamb', which turned out to be an extremely fatty breast of that animal, with peas and new potatoes from the garden.

It was apparent from the infrequent entertaining that was done, that this would be the last occasion when Nelly would be called upon to demonstrate her art, so she swallowed her pride and set about making the best of a cut of meat which she despised.

Winnie Bailey, Ella Bembridge and Dotty Harmer were coming to lunch, and the amount of meat available, in Nelly's opinion, would just about feed two, rather than six. She herself had said swiftly that she was obliged to have something light, and would prefer a dry biscuit and a small piece of cheese if that was all right?

Miss Ada graciously gave her consent, and with her own hands put two water biscuits and about a quarter of an ounce of dessicated Cheddar cheese on a plate, and put it in the larder for Nelly's repast.

Nelly contrived to make a substantial stuffing of onions, bread crumbs and herbs, and rolled the breast of lamb, hoping that the guests had had large breakfasts.

'And welcome they are to *that*,' said Nelly, to the attentive cat, as she thrust the meat tin into the oven, and then set about making a bread pudding, sparsely furnished with a few sultanas which Miss Ada had counted out earlier.

As she handed round the vegetables at lunch time, she listened to the conversation with much interest. Dotty Harmer's dog, Flossie, was the subject of much questioning.

'I'm afraid so,' said Dotty. 'The vet said she could be aborted, but I don't like the idea.'

'Of what?' asked Miss Violet, who was slightly deaf.

'Of *abortion*,' shouted Dotty.

'*Pas devant la bonne*,' murmured Miss Ada, but Dotty was in no mood for such niceties.

'Why not?' she demanded. 'Abortion is a perfectly normal medical fact. Not, as I said before, that I approve of it. I told the vet that Flossie must just go ahead and have them. I am quite capable of looking after her, and her offspring, and I'm sure I shall find good homes for them.'

She cast speculative glances upon her fellow guests, who quailed. Dotty, with animals to place, was rightly feared by all Lulling and Thrush Green.

'I'm quite sure you will,' said Miss Bertha soothingly. 'If we weren't so near the road, and were more capable of giving a puppy exercise, I'm sure we might have offered to have one.'

'But as it is,' chimed in Miss Ada, 'it is quite out of the question.'

'Indeed it is,' agreed Miss Violet.

'The pudding, Nelly. Would you see if it is ready?' requested Miss Ada, and Nelly was obliged to leave this fascinating conversation and return to the kitchen.

'It's like a mad house in there,' she confided to the cat. 'Well-bred they might be—all six of 'em—but they sound half-barmy to me, the things they talk about!'

*   *   *

At the village school, unconfined joy reigned. It was the last day of term.

In Miss Fogerty's new classroom the cupboards were packed to bursting point with books, folders and boxes belonging to the children. Other, less obliging shapes, such as hanks of raffia, snarls of cane and balls of wet clay swathed in damp dish-cloths, were also tidied away, with considerable difficulty, into their allotted place.

As always, just as Miss Fogerty, breathless with lodging the last object into the last space, was about to congratulate herself on finishing an awkward and arduous job, one of the children drew her attention to half a dozen large flower vases which should be stowed away.

'They will have to stay on the windowsill,' decreed Agnes. 'Stand them by the fish tank, dear, and you, Jimmy Todd, may go early with the goldfish so that your bucket isn't jogged by anyone on the way home.'

Jimmy Todd, the envy of the class, had a fish tank of his own, and was to look after Freeman, Hardy and Willis for the entire holiday.

'I *hope*,' little Miss Fogerty had confided to Miss Watson, 'I *sincerely hope* that the boy is trustworthy. He is inclined to be a trifle irresponsible at times.'

'He is only seven,' pointed out her headmistress. 'But there's no need to think that he is not perfectly capable of caring for the fish. He has sensible parents, and a little responsibility may work wonders for him.'

Miss Fogerty had her doubts. Secretly, she deplored handing out responsible jobs, such as fish minding and blackboard cleaning, to those who had not earned the honour by worthy

and decorous behaviour, but as Jimmy Todd was the only child with a spare fish tank she bowed to the inevitable.

He was sent on his way ten minutes before the others, plastic bucket in hand and fervent protestations of concern for his charges on his lips. Miss Fogerty's last glimpse of him was at the school gates where he had stopped to peer anxiously through the butter muslin which Miss Fogerty had tied over the top of the pail.

She gave a sigh of relief.

'I'm sure they will be quite safe with Jimmy,' she said aloud.

'Jimmy Todd,' said a child in the front row, 'has got three cats as likes fish.'

Miss Fogerty quelled her with a glance.

'All stand. Hands together. Close your eyes. *Close* them, I said, Billy Bates, not *cross* them! Any silly nonsense like that, and you stay in, last day of term or not!'

Fortunately, Miss Fogerty's discipline held, and prayers were said reverently. It was as well, she thought, bidding the children goodbye, as she was due to go to tea with Isobel in five minutes' time.

The hot weather continued, day after day, week after week. The heat was almost overpowering as Agnes made her way to Tullivers, thankful for the deep shade of the chestnut avenue.

'One could really do with a parasol,' she said to Isobel, when they were seated in the shade with the tea-tray before them. 'My grandmother had a beautiful cream one, with lace and frills, I remember. Those Victorians had some excellent ideas.'

'My grandmother,' said Isobel, 'had a dove-grey silk one, and the knob on the handle was of pink china, with a tiny picture of Brighton Pier at the top. I wonder where that went eventually?'

'To a jumble sale, no doubt,' responded Agnes, accepting a teacup.

'And now tell me what you are doing this holiday,' said Isobel. 'I know you have been invited to go to the sea with Miss Watson. Is that soon?'

'She goes next Saturday. Her brother and his wife are taking her down, and staying for a week in this nice quiet hotel that Dorothy likes at Barton-on-Sea. Then I'm going down for the next week, while Ray goes with Kathleen to her sister's, and then they are bringing us both back here.'

'It will do you good to have some sea air, especially if the weather holds.'

'It will do Dorothy good too. There are some nice flat cliff top walks which she can manage now, and easy paths down to the sands.'

'And after that?'

'I shall have a week or so here catching up with all sorts of things I've been meaning to do, and then I shall spend a few days at my cousin's at Cheltenham.'

'And I hope a few days with me if you can spare the time,' said Isobel. 'As far as I can see, I shall be going back before long, and this may be the last time I can offer you hospitality in Sussex. With any luck, I shall have found something near here very soon, and it will be a joy to be near you permanently.'

'I should love to come,' said Agnes, and meant it. Isobel's home was as luxurious as her own bed-sitting-room was spartan. Not that she was discontented with her lot. She had been with the Whites now for a number of years, and appreciated their high standards of cleanliness and responsibility, and their kindness on the rare occasions when she had been obliged to stay in bed because of ill-health.

But it was good to exchange her skimpy bedclothes for Isobel's fluffy blankets and fat eiderdown. It was bliss to have a soft bath towel large enough to envelope her whole body, and wonderful to have exquisite meals served on Isobel's pretty china, instead of on the thick white plates from Mrs White's kitchen.

And then there was the warmth of Isobel's company to

enliven her. There had never been anyone quite so dear to her as Isobel, and she enjoyed every minute of her company. Indeed, it had crossed her mind once, when Isobel had first mentioned that she wanted to live near Thrush Green, that she might be invited to share Isobel's home. But, on the whole, she was glad that the matter had not arisen.

Isobel had so many friends already at Thrush Green, and would soon make many more. Agnes did not want her to feel obliged to invite her to meet them, as no doubt Isobel would do. It would be a *strain*, thought Agnes, to have to be sociable when one arrived home, jaded from school, longing simply for a rest with one's feet up, and a quiet cup of tea. Besides, it had to be faced, Isobel's circle of friends was not quite her own. No, it was far better as it was—to visit Isobel in her own home, when she had found it, and to remain in her own modest lodgings which suited her very well. Of course, she was lonely at times, she admitted, but then one simply had to get used to it. There were plenty of single women in the same circumstances and, on the whole, they were certainly better off than those poor unfortunate women who had made unhappy marriages, she told herself stoutly.

But then she was more fortunate than most. The future looked bright. Dear Dorothy was fast returning to health and mobility, and she would always be grateful to her for giving her this lovely week's holiday which lay ahead. 'A small return, Agnes dear, for more kindness than I can ever repay,' is how she had put it.

And then, beyond that, lay the happy prospect of having Iosbel actually living at Thrush Green!

Little Miss Fogerty lay back in her deck-chair, and gazed

at Tullivers' flowers shimmering in the heat. She was at peace with the world.

Joan Young soon had a reply to her letter. There was nothing they would love more, wrote Molly, than to live in the top flat of the house which had always seemed like home to her.

Ben could not believe in such luck, and was now waiting to hear from the Collets which day they would like to interview him. Reading between the lines, Joan gathered that he was in a high state of tension, poor fellow, and hoped that his ordeal would soon be over. So much depended upon it, he was bound to be nervous.

He did not have to wait long. About ten days later, Molly, Ben and young George arrived at Lulling. Molly and George went to Albert Piggott's gloomy cottage while Ben, dressed in his best blue serge suit, and his dark hair brushed flat against his head, went to see Tim Collet, his heart beating nineteen to the dozen.

Nelly was at her Lulling job, and Molly prepared midday dinner for the three of them, her mind engrossed with what was happening at Lulling. As soon as they had eaten, and she had washed up, she took George out of the way, before Nelly returned, and sat on one of the many seats on Thrush Green.

The excessive heat had scorched the grass, and even the fully-grown trees were beginning to look parched and dusty. But there were a few daisies about, and a friendly collie dog, and these kept young George happily engaged, leaving Molly free to ponder on the joys that might be ahead.

From where she sat, she had a clear view of the top of the

hill, and longed to see their old van arrive with Ben at the wheel.

To her left lay the golden bulk of the Youngs' house, beyond the chestnut trees and the railings which ran along the front of the house. She could hear the noise of the builders at work, the chink of metal on stone, the rumble of a wheelbarrow, and an occasional voice as one workman shouted to another.

If only they could live there! If only Ben had landed this job! She began to tremble at the thought of failure. It would be like getting to the gate of heaven and being turned back. There was nowhere in the world that she wanted to be more. This was home. This was her element, as necessary to her as air to a bird, or water to a fish. Without it she would be nothing, simply an adjunct to Ben's life, going where he went, and making the best of any of the places in which he settled.

But here, at Thrush Green, life would be rich and vital. She and Ben would flourish like plants in a sheltered garden, and George would grow up in perfect surroundings, heir to all the joys of Thrush Green.

The sound of the van chugging up the hill sent her flying across the grass, followed by young George.

There was no need to say anything. Ben's glowing face said it all.

'Oh Ben!' cried Molly, clinging to him, and struggling to control tears of relief.

Ben patted her shoulder.

'There! Let's go straight across to Mrs Young, Moll, and tell her the good news.'

19 Miss Fogerty has a Shock

NELLY PIGGOTT faced her last day's work at the Lovelocks' with mingled relief and apprehension.

The job had been a frustrating one. It was not only poorly paid, but the parsimony of her employers had tried Nelly's patience to breaking point. It had been a considerable effort to hold her tongue under such extreme provocation, and only the thought of the comparatively short time she needed to endure it, had kept her from outspoken rebellion. No, she would not be sorry to leave this post.

On the other hand, the outlook for any other work seemed bleak. This puzzled Nelly. She was known as a good worker and an exceptionally fine cook. Why was it that she was unable to land another job?

She had haunted the Job Centre. She had asked a dozen or more Thrush Green and Lulling folk if they knew of a job, but always there was some difficulty. One of the reasons, Nelly felt sure, was her past flightiness. Lulling did not approve of wives leaving their husbands, even such unpleasant ones as Albert Piggott, to run off with oil men as glossy and dashing as the one who had persuaded Nelly to throw in her lot with his.

There were other reasons too. Most of the people who were lucky enough to have domestic aid, had employed their helpers for years, as Winnie Bailey had her Jenny, and Dotty Harmer and Harold Shoosmith their energetic Betty Bell. Others, who might have looked for help in the past, had long ago come to terms with doing everything for themselves and had found the result far more satisfactory, and far less expensive. One way and another, it was plain that there were no jobs waiting for Nelly.

As she returned to her house on Thrush Green, on the last afternoon of her employment, Nelly took stock of her position. Financially, she was a little better off than when she had arrived at Thrush Green. Prudently, she had put aside the money she had earned in her Post Office account. By diligent methods, she had been able to abstract some money from Albert, ostensibly for housekeeping, but a certain amount had been added to her own nest egg.

She owned an ancient gold watch, and a gold locket of hideous Victorian design, and these she knew would bring in a pound or two, if she were really hard pressed. The point was, could she afford to break with Albert?

She had long ceased to feel for him any affection or loyalty, but he did provide a roof over her head and enough to feed them both. But he grew daily more cantankerous, and Nelly knew that, before long, just such another row as that which had sent her into the arms of the oil man would blow up.

Crossing the green, Nelly decided that she would give Albert a week's trial. Who knows? Work might turn up to take her out of the house for a few hours a day. Albert might become a reformed character, though that chance was infinitesimal.

She would bide her time for a little longer, and then make her decision.

Albert was emerging from the Two Pheasants as Nelly opened the cottage door. For once, she did not start nagging at him.

Albert was rightly suspicious. What was up, he wondered?

On the appointed Saturday, Miss Watson was collected by her brother and his wife, and departed to the seaside.

Little Miss Fogerty had made her farewells the evening before as she helped Dorothy with her last-minute packing. Watching her assistant's deftness in folding garments and spreading tissue paper, Dorothy thought, once more, how invaluable dear Agnes was, and how dearly she would like to invite her to share the schoolhouse. Perhaps an opportunity would occur during their week together, but, on the other hand, there was always this difficulty of Agnes's unselfishness. If only the suggestion could come from her!

Well, it was no good worrying about it, thought Miss Watson, limping towards the car on that bright morning. Time alone could unravel that problem, and meanwhile she intended to enjoy her much-needed change of air.

Meanwhile, Miss Fogerty set about a number of jobs which she had been unable to tackle during term time.

The position of temporary headmistress, in which Miss Watson's sad accident had placed her, had meant putting aside a great many day to day activities which she normally tackled methodically.

Her mending, for instance, which was usually done after ironing, when she studied her sensible underwear and blouses for splitting seams, holes, ladders or missing buttons, had been neglected. The filling of innumerable forms had taken first place, and there had been parents, representatives from educational publishers, and other visitors to the school, who seriously impeded the steady progress of the work which Agnes so much enjoyed.

Now was the time to catch up with her own affairs, and she spent the next day or two replying to letters from friends, doing some shopping, taking shoes to the repairer's, and all the other little chores which she wanted to see finished before embarking on the longed-for week with Dorothy.

But two days before the great day, poor Miss Fogerty received the shock of her life. St Andrew's clock had just chimed four o'clock, and Miss Fogerty was about to switch on her kettle and make a cup of tea, when Mrs White called from below to say that she had just made a pot of tea, and would she like to join her?

It was while they were sipping the refreshing beverage in Mrs White's immaculate sitting-room, that the blow fell.

'I've been trying to summon up courage to tell you all the week,' confessed Mrs White. 'Arthur's got promotion, and we're moving to Scotland.'

Her face turned pink with the anxiety of imparting this news. Poor Miss Fogerty's turned white at hearing it.

She put down her cup with a clatter.

'Oh no!' she breathed at last. 'I can't believe it! You mean —?'

'I'm afraid so,' nodded Mrs White, beginning to look tearful. 'I can't tell you how sorry I am about it. You've been a wonderful lodger, and a real good friend too, but Arthur can't afford to turn down this chance. It'll make a deal of difference to his pension, you see.'

'Of course,' said Agnes. She felt numbed with the shock. What a terrible thing to happen! How soon, she wondered, would she need to go?

As if reading her thoughts, Mrs White resumed her tale.

'There's no need for you to worry about leaving just yet. We don't go until the end of August, and Arthur's job starts on the first of September. There's a house that goes with it, and with the extra he'll get we hope to be able to buy our own house, ready for retirement one day.'

Agnes did her best to collect her scattered wits.

'I'm very glad for you both,' she said sincerely. 'The future certainly looks bright. It's just that I'm a little taken aback, you know, and at a loss to know where to find other lodgings. I doubt if I shall ever be so happy elsewhere as I have been with you.'

Mrs White sighed with relief.

'You've taken it wonderfully. I can't tell you how I've dreaded breaking the news.'

She turned briskly to her duties as hostess.

'Now let me give you a fresh cup of tea. That must be stone cold by now.'

Like my heart, thought poor Agnes, doing her best to hide her feelings. What on earth would she do now?

Later that evening, she went along the road to Thrush Green and called to see Isobel at Tullivers.

Her old friend was alone, and Agnes poured out all her troubles. Isobel was almost as upset as she was herself.

'If only I had found a place here,' was her first comment, 'you could have taken refuge with me. The awful thing is, Agnes dear, I shall probably be back in Sussex by the time you need another home. Does Mrs White know of other digs?'

'She didn't say anything.'

'Could you stay at the schoolhouse?'

'I'm sure Dorothy would let me stay there temporarily, if need be, but I really must find something permanent.'

'If I were you,' said Isobel, 'I should go and enjoy your holiday, and then come back to face this problem. The best thing to do, I think, would be to put an advertisement in the local paper, as soon as you return.'

'I thought I might tell the rector. He's so kind. He helped with finding a place for you with Miss Bembridge, you remember, and he would know the sort of place I wanted.'

'An excellent idea! I'm positive something will turn up before the end of August. Meanwhile, Agnes, you are going to stay to supper with me, I hope.'

'I can think of nothing nicer,' said little Miss Fogerty, much comforted.

The intense heat ended, as expected, with a crashing' thunderstorm which began at seven in the evening and continued for most of the night.

The people of Lulling and Thrush Green waited eagerly for the rain to fall. Water-butts stood empty, flowers wilted, the summer pea pods were shrivelled on their stems, and even the farmers, now that the harvest was largely gathered in, looked forward to a downpour.

For some hours it looked as though nothing would fall. Crash followed crash, angry rumblings echoed round the sky, and sheet lightning lit the scene with eerie flashes, but still the rain held off. It was almost midnight before the welcome sound of pattering drops cheered the waiting inhabitants.

The relief was wonderful. The delicious smell of rain water cooling hot stones and earth was then more appreciated than the most expensive scent. Rain splashed on the parched grass of Thrush Green, and pattered on the great dusty leaves of the chestnut trees. It gurgled down the gutters to Lulling, and formed wide puddles across the road outside St Andrew's church. It sent the local cats, out upon their nightly forays, scampering for home, and encouraged the thirsty wild creatures to venture forth for their first satisfying drink for many a long day.

The air grew blessedly cool and fresh. The wakeful ones sought those blankets which had been unused for weeks, and snuggled into their beds with thankful hearts.

The morning after the storm dawned clear and fresh. The world of Thrush Green sparkled in the sunshine, and everyone relished the slight coolness in the air, and the rejuvenation of all living things.

Even Albert Piggott gave the green a grudging smile as he walked across to St Andrew's. Here he proposed to spend a leisurely hour or two surveying his domain, safe from Nelly's gaze.

Nelly had finished at the Lovelocks', and mightily relieved she was to be able to set to and do her own chores without one eye on the clock. The Misses Lovelock had been sticklers for punctuality, and would not have been above docking Nelly's wages if she had arrived late. Knowing this, Nelly had been very particular in arriving promptly.

She had been paid in full, and wished goodbye by all three ladies. Miss Ada had been gracious enough to say that she would be willing to supply a reference if Nelly required it at any time. Nelly thanked her civilly.

The snag was that there was still no work available, and the thought of being at close quarters with Albert, day in and day out, was a daunting one.

She thought about her future as she dismantled the stove and prepared to scour each part in strong soda water. Albert had been at his grumpiest for the past week. The truth was that he disliked the heat, and that Nelly's cooking was again playing havoc with his digestion. He enjoyed venting his ill-humour upon Nelly, and during the thunderstorm whilst they were hoping for rain, he had been particularly unpleasant about Nelly's chances of employment.

'Can't expect decent folks to take on a trollop like you,' was the phrase that hurt most. It still rankled as Nelly attacked the cooker. The thing was, it was near the truth, and Nelly knew it.

She began to think of Charlie, the oil man. With all his faults, he had never been unkind to her, or insulted her as Albert did. Looking back now, she forgot his meanness, his dishonesty with money, and the long evenings she had spent alone, trying to keep his supper hot without it spoiling.

She thought of his attractions, his glossy black hair, the music hall ditties he was so fond of singing, and the good times they had enjoyed together at local pubs. True to her principles, Nelly had stuck to bitter lemon or orange juice while Charlie swigged his whisky, but she had enjoyed meeting his rowdy friends and joining in the songs around the bar piano.

She paused in her scrubbing and gazed out of the steamy window towards Thrush Green. Not much life here, that was for sure! And what would it be like in the winter, when the curtains were drawn at four o'clock, and Albert had left her for the Two Pheasants next door? A living death, decided Nelly, just a living death!

She would have done better to have looked for a place where she was. There was far more scope for her talents in Brighton than ever there would be at Thrush Green. She pondered the matter for a full hour, by which time the cooker had been reassembled, and the frying-pan filled with bacon, liver and sausages for the midday meal.

'Fatty stuff again, I see,' grunted Albert, when his plate was put before him later. 'You knows what Doctor Lovell said. You trying to kill me?'

'Chance'd be a fine thing,' retorted Nelly. 'The devil looks after his own, as far as I can see.'

Albert snorted.

'You'd be a far sight fitter,' went on Nelly, 'if you laid off the beer. All that acid fair eats away the lining of your stummick. I was reading about it in my women's paper.'

'You wants to change the record,' snarled Albert, with heavy sarcasm. 'And if you looked for a job instead of wastin' your time with women's papers you'd be a bit better off.'

Nelly rose from the table with as much dignity as a sixteen stone woman could manage, and went to the dresser drawer. From it she abstracted a cheap packet of stationery and a ballpoint pen, and made her way upstairs.

Sitting on the side of the spare bed she composed a letter to Charlie. It was not an easy letter to write, and how it would be received was anybody's guess. It took Nelly nearly an hour to get her thoughts on paper, and when at last she had sealed the envelope and stuck on the stamp, she descended the stairs.

Albert was fast asleep in the armchair. His mouth was open, and he snored loudly, making a maddening little whining sound as he did so. The dirty dishes still littered the table, and the newly-cleaned stove bore fresh splashes of fat.

Nelly opened the door, and marched straight across the grass to the post-box on the corner of Thrush Green. She was oblivious of the fresh beauty about her, and the bright new world which the rain had created.

She dropped the letter in the box, and heard its satisfying plop as it reached the bottom.

Well, she'd done it! She'd burnt her boats, thought Nelly, and now she must face the future!

20 A Proposal

MISS FOGERTY travelled by coach from Thrush Green to Bournemouth where she was being met. She determined to take Isobel's advice and postpone all thoughts of finding new accommodation until she returned, but she had called on Charles Henstock, before she left for her week's holiday, and told him of her predicament.

'My dear Miss Fogerty,' said that kind man, his chubby face creased with concern, 'I shall do my very best to find somewhere for you. Try not to let it worry you when you are away. You need a break after all the troubles of last term. Something will turn up, I feel convinced.'

He had told his wife about the encounter, and Dimity at once thought of Ella.

'The only thing is she has said so little about taking a lodger recently, that I'm beginning to wonder if she really wants one.'

'We can only ask,' said Charles. 'Perhaps you could broach the subject?'

Dimity did, that very afternoon, and as she had surmised, Ella did not appear at all keen.

'The point is, Dim, I've been thinking it over, and I've got quite used to being alone here, and I'm not all that hard up. I mean, look at my clothes!'

Dimity looked, and was secretly appalled.

'I've had these trousers five years, and this shirt much the same length of time, and I can't see myself bothering to buy much in that line. And then I don't go out as much as I used to, nor do the same amount of entertaining as we did when you were here. One way and another, I think I'd sooner scratch along on my own.'

'But you thoroughly enjoyed having Isobel,' Dimity pointed out.

'Isobel's one in a thousand and in any case it was only for a week. I just don't want anyone permanently.'

'In a way,' said Dimity, 'I'm relieved to hear it.'

'Not that I'd see little Agnes homeless,' continued Ella. 'If she hasn't found anywhere before term starts, I'm very willing to put her up for a bit while she's looking round. I'm fond of that funny little soul.'

'We all are,' replied Dimity.

It was soon after this, that Harold walked across to Tullivers to tell Isobel that he had ordered an Alfa Romeo very like her own, and was now bracing himself to part with the ancient Daimler which had played an important part in his life.

The day was cool and cloudy. In fact, the violent thunder storm had brought the hot summer weather to an end, and there were to be very few sunny days until the autumn.

He found Isobel busy writing letters. She gave him her usual warm smile which affected his heart in such a delightful way, but he thought that she appeared somewhat worried.

'Anything wrong?' he asked, seating himself at the table where her writing things were littered.

Isobel put her hands flat on the table with a gesture of despair.

'A lot, I'm afraid. I was coming to tell you. I shall have to drive home again. There's a muddle about the sale of the house.'

'Can't the estate agent cope with that? Must you go today?'

'Either today, or tomorrow morning. The sale's fallen through again.'

She sighed, and looked so desperately unhappy, that Harold could not bear it. He had never seen her cast down. In all their fruitless searchings for a house she had always managed to maintain a certain buoyancy of spirit which was one of the reasons why he loved her.

He put a hand over one of hers, and spoke urgently.

'Isobel, let me help with this. I can't bear to see you so unhappy, and it's all so unnecessary.'

'Unnecessary?' queried Isobel.

'I've wanted to say something for weeks now, but it has never seemed the right moment. I don't know if this is— but hear me out, Isobel, I beg of you.'

He tightened his grip on her hand, and began his plea. Isobel sat very still, her eyes downcast upon their linked hands, and heard him out as he had asked.

'And will you?' he ended. 'Could'you, Isobel?'

She smiled at him, and at last regained her hand.

'Thank you, Harold dear. You must let me think for a day or so. My mind is so confused with all that's happened, I shall need time. But I do thank you, from the bottom of my heart. It is the loveliest thing that has happened to me for a long, long time.'

'You dear girl!' exclaimed Harold. 'And please don't keep me waiting too long! I warn you, I've been in a state of near-dementia for the past months.'

Isobel laughed. 'I promise you an answer before the end of the week, but I must get back and sort out some of this muddle. Oh, the misery of selling and buying houses!'

'You know the way out now,' Harold pointed out.

'You would never know,' replied Isobel, 'if I'd married you or the house.'

'I'll take that risk,' Harold assured her.

As always, the building activity at the Youngs' took considerably longer than had at first been imagined, despite Edward's daily exhortations.

To be fair, the builders worked well, but there were interminable delays in getting materials from the suppliers which held up the proceedings.

It was plain that the top flat was going to be ready before the stable block conversion, but even so it did not look as though the second bedroom would be ready in time for the Curdles' arrival in September.

Joan wrote to let them know how things were, and was glad to hear that the negotiations for the sale of the fair to Dick Hasler were now almost completed. They would be selling their caravan home when they came to Thrush Green, wrote Molly, and the money would help them to furnish the flat.

But, asked Molly, Ben could not bear to part with his grandmother's wooden gipsy caravan, and could they bring it with them? Would there be somewhere out of the way where it could stand? It might be quite a useful spare-room, and Ben would be very pleased if they would like to use it as such at any time in the future.

Joan felt a surge of happiness when she read this. What could be better? Mrs Curdle's much-loved caravan had always been an important part of Thrush Green's life. May the first had been the highlight of the year, and it was only fitting that the caravan should return to its old haunt forever, and to stand close to the last resting place of its famous owner.

'There's plenty of room in the orchard,' Edward said, when he heard about the proposal. He was as delighted as Joan to think of having the caravan at Thrush Green.

So were their neighbours and friends. Winnie Bailey, in particular, welcomed the idea, remembering how old Mrs Curdle had visited her regularly every year.

'It's so much part of Thrush Green history,' said the rector, summing up general opinion, 'that it's the *only* place for it. We shall all treasure it.'

Nelly Piggott awaited an answer to her letter with some anxiety. For one thing, she wanted to take it from the postman as soon as it arrived. No one could accuse Albert of undue interest in the meagre correspondence which was slipped under the door, but he might well open a letter which was written by hand thinking it might be from Molly, who was about the only person who did write to him.

Manilla envelopes, with typed addresses, were beneath his notice. They would either contain bills, or some other objectionable enclosures, which would be stowed, often unopened, behind the clock on the kitchen mantel shelf, for later perusal.

Nelly was usually up first, and downstairs by the time Willie Bond delivered the post. If Willie Bond was on duty, he arrived whilst Nelly was on her own in the kitchen.

But if the second postman, Willie Marchant, delivered the mail then he arrived a good half-hour later, and by then Albert was at large in the kitchen with her.

A fortnight had passed and still there was no response from the oil man. Of course, Nelly told herself, he might be away. He might even have moved house, but in that case, surely he would have left an address at the Post Office, and his letters would have been forwarded.

It was more likely, Nelly was bound to admit, that he did not consider a reply necessary, and did not intend to waste good money on a stamp for one who had upped and left him comparatively recently.

'Can't blame him, I suppose,' said Nelly to Albert's cat,

when Willie Bond had departed after leaving a seed catalogue addressed to Albert, the only item of mail.

But it was worrying. It would be better to know the worst. It would be *far* better, Nelly told herself, to have a rude letter telling her what he thought of her, than this horrible silence.

During this waiting period she had cleaned the house from top to bottom. Any object which could be assaulted with strong soda water, yellow soap and a stiff scrubbingbrush, had been so treated. Anything which could be polished, whether it were of metal, wood or glass, had been attacked mercilessly. Even the cat, once so thin, had been fattened with Nelly's good food, and was given a brisk brushing, and its ears cleaned out with oily cotton wool twisted into a serviceable radish shape.

In between these frenzied spells of cleaning, Nelly took short walks. Sometimes, in order to get away from Albert, she took herself to Lulling and surveyed the shops, or called at the Job Centre, in case she would need to earn again. Sometimes, she strolled towards Lulling Woods, and once went as far as the Drovers' Arms and called on the Allens, secretly hoping that there might be work for her there, if the oil man did not come up to scratch. But there was nothing there, as the Allens made clear, softening the blow by giving her a cup of tea and Garibaldi biscuits, before she made the return journey.

Albert was more melancholy than ever, and Nelly was beginning to wonder how much longer she could stand the suspense of waiting, and the tedium of her husband's nagging.

When, one happy morning, Willie Marchant handed in the letter she had been waiting for, she was able to put it quickly into her overall pocket before Albert realised what was going on.

When he had departed to his duties at St Andrew's, she

opened the envelope. The letter was short and to the point:

> Dear Nelly,
>> Come on back, you old faggot.
>> Forgiven and forgotten.
>>> Love,
>>>> Charlie

Nelly could have wept with relief. There was a man for you! Big-hearted, took life as it came, willing to forget and forgive! She wouldn't leave him again in a hurry, that was sure! Why, he'd even put 'Love' at the end! No doubt about it, Charlie was one in a million!

She sat down at the kitchen table and wrote back. Her letter was even more brief than Charlie's:

> Darling Charlie,
>> Coming Wednesday,
>>> Best love,
>>> Your Nelly

She had to walk down the hill to Lulling to buy a stamp, but she was too happy to mind. Normally, she found the return journey, up the steep hill, distinctly daunting, but on this occasion she sailed up it as blithely as a Lakeland fell climber.

Life was about to start again for Nelly Piggott.

At Barton-on-sea Agnes and Dorothy sat on the veranda of the small hotel, and admired the sea.

It was still difficult for Dorothy to negotiate the steps nearest to the hotel, leading to the beach, and the weather was not as reliable as one could wish for a seaside holiday. The veranda gave them shelter from the wind, and all the sunshine that was available.

'Besides, dear,' Miss Watson pointed out, 'here we are handy for our library books and knitting, or a cup of coffee, if we want it. And sand can be rather *pervasive*. Into everything, isn't it? But don't let me stop you, Agnes, if you want to have a walk along the beach. I'm quite happy here.'

Agnes assured her that she was perfectly contented.

'We'll have a little stroll along the cliff top later,' said Dorothy. 'Grass is so much pleasanter to walk on than sand.'

Miss Fogerty agreed automatically. It was wonderful to be here, taking in the fresh salt-laden air, feeling the warmth of the sun, and the comfort of Dorothy's presence. But her mind still fluttered round her problem, despite her determination to shelve it, as advised by dear Isobel and Charles Henstock. It was easier said than done.

For two days now she had fought against the temptation to confide in her headmistress. Agnes had always found it difficult to keep anything from her. By nature she was not a secretive person, although she could be discreet with other people's confidences.

She gazed out to the sparkling sea, watching the gulls swoop and scream, as they swerved for food being thrown to them by someone hidden from her sight below the cliff. Involuntarily, she sighed.

Miss Watson was quick to notice.

'Agnes dear, are you *sure* you want to sit here? Do say if you feel like doing anything else. I want this little holiday to be *exactly* as you want it. I shall feel *most unhappy* if I am holding you back.'

'Indeed, Dorothy, I am doing just what I want,' cried Agnes.

'But you don't seem quite yourself,' replied Dorothy solicitously. 'Are you quite well? Are you worried about anything? Surely you can tell an old friend any troubles?'

Her kind face, peering so anxiously into that of her companion's, was Agnes Fogerty's undoing.

The floodgates opened, and the whole pitiful story poured forth. Mr White's promotion, his pension, his savings, Mrs White's reluctance to tell her lodger, her tact in doing so, her past kindnesses, all flowed from Agnes in a stream of words, to which Dorothy listened with mingled pity and hope.

'And so,' concluded Agnes, having recourse to one of her best Swiss handkerchiefs, 'I must look for something else. I didn't mean to tell you, you know. It isn't fair to unload my troubles on you when you are still convalescent.'

Miss Watson took a deep breath of good sea air.

'I don't consider myself *convalescent* any longer,' she said robustly. 'And you have taken a great weight off my mind.'

'I have?' quavered Agnes.

'You see, I dearly wanted to ask you if you would consider living permanently at the schoolhouse. There's nothing I should like more, but I feared you might feel I was in need and your unselfishness would prompt you to do something which perhaps you did not really want to do.'

'Not really want to do?' echoed Agnes.

'You must think it over,' went on Dorothy. 'I shall quite understand if you refuse. I know that your independence means a lot to you, and I respect that. I respect it very much.'

Little Miss Fogerty returned her handkerchief to her pocket, and sat up very straight.

'I don't need any time, Dorothy, to think it over. To live at the schoolhouse would please me more than anything in the world, if you're *really sure.*'

'I've been *really sure* for months,' said Dorothy. 'And now I think we might celebrate in that cup of coffee, Agnes dear, if you can reach the bell.'

At Thrush Green, Harold Shoosmith awaited Isobel's answer with anxious impatience. She had been gone for three days now, and he was sure that she would keep her promise and let him know within the week. But what a ghastly length of time that seemed!

Neither Willie Bond, nor Willie Marchant, had ever seen him so swift to take in the letters. The telephone receiver was snatched from the cradle before it had time to ring twice, and Harold was remarkably short with those who rang up. After all, it might be the very moment that Isobel was trying to get through.

Betty Bell noted his agitation with some sympathy and amusement.

'I bet you miss Mrs Fletcher,' she remarked conversationally, over elevenses.

Harold ignored the remark.

'A real nice lady,' continued Betty, crunching a ginger biscuit. 'Miss Harmer was only saying yesterday as how it would be lovely to have her living here.'

'Here?' interjected Harold. Was it so obvious?

'In Thrush Green,' explained Betty. 'Or nearby. Everyone wants her back.'

Not as much as I do, thought Harold, pushing back his chair.

'Well, I must get on with my hedge-cutting,' said Harold, making his escape.

It was Betty Bell who answered the telephone half an hour later.

'Hang on,' she shouted cheerfully. 'I'll get him.'

She hung out of the kitchen window.

'Mrs Fletcher on the phone,' she yelled, and admired the speed with which her employer abandoned the shears and sprinted up the path.

She would dearly have loved to listen to the conversation on the bedroom extension, but decided to retreat to the landing where, with any luck, she would be out of sight, and might hear at least one side of the proceedings.

She had to wait some time, for there seemed to be a great deal said at the Sussex end, but at last her vigil was rewarded.

'Oh, Isobel!' cried her employer. 'You darling! Yes, I'll be with you at twelve tomorrow, with a bottle of champagne.'

There was another break, and then: 'I can't say all I want to, but I'll say it tomorrow. Yes, Betty's here, and listening too, I've no doubt. But who cares?'

When a minute later he put down the telephone, Betty sauntered down the stairs with as convincing an air of innocence as she could muster.

'Betty,' said Harold, his face radiant. 'I'm going to get married.'

'Really, sir?'

'To Mrs Fletcher,' said Harold.

'We all said you would,' said Betty, picking up her duster.

Epilogue

Epilogue

ONE golden October morning, Robert and Milly Bassett at last arrived at Thrush Green.

The air was crisp and clear, and the sky that pellucid blue which only early autumn brings. The chestnut leaves were turning colour, and some had already fallen, spreading a glowing, crackling carpet beneath the trees.

Over lunch, Joan had plenty to tell her parents. There were still several things to finish at their new home, and Joan insisted that they slept in the old house until she was satisfied that the new plaster had dried out.

Otherwise, the stable block had become a charming one-storey house, sheltered by the Cotswold stone garden wall, and shaded by mature trees. Robert and Milly were delighted with it.

'And how about Ben and Molly?' asked Milly. 'How's the new job going?'

'Splendidly. He's so happy, and Tim Collet told Edward that he'll probably put him into a more responsible job when one of the older men leaves after Christmas.'

'And Molly?'

'As helpful as ever, and relieved to be near her father, of course, especially now that Nelly's left him.'

'It's little George I want to see,' said Milly.

'He's at school now, with Miss Fogerty. He was promoted to filling in the weather chart this week, so you can see he's happy enough!'

The Hursts were back, Joan told them, and Frank had evidently made a great hit with his lecture tour, and had been invited to go again the following year.

'But our most exciting news,' said Joan, when she poured the coffee, 'is of Harold Shoosmith. He's on his honeymoon at the moment, and you can guess the flutter his marriage made here.'

'Better late than never,' pronounced Robert. 'And he couldn't have chosen more wisely.'

Obedient to the directions of his wife and daughter, Robert went to lie down for an hour and, to his surprise, had a short nap. The journey must have tired him more than he realised.

Much refreshed, he rose and made his way into the garden, and wandered among the falling leaves, admiring the Michaelmas daisies, the golden rod, and the velvet brilliance of the dahlias. It was a lovely time of year to come home, he thought, and sighed with pleasure.

He turned into the orchard and caught his breath with delight. There, beneath a gnarled apple tree, stood dear Mrs Curdle's caravan. Joan had not mentioned this, and he went to investigate.

It was in excellent trim. The paint was fresh, the brass polished, the minute windows sparkling.

The top half of the door was open, and Robert could see that it looked just as he remembered it in Mrs Curdle's day. There was the shining stove, the framed text above it, and the gaudy counterpane smoothed over the bunk bed.

It gave Robert enormous joy to see the little home again, and he was smiling as he retraced his steps.

He went out of the open front gate and surveyed the scene.

On his right was the village school. The younger children were already emerging from the new classroom at the back of the playground, George, no doubt, among them. In the distance, he could see little Agnes Fogerty, and waved to her.

She waved back, and he thought what a splendid thing it was that she and Miss Watson had joined forces. Nothing like a little companionship as you grew older!

Beside the school, Harold's house stood with its windows closed, awaiting the return of its master and new mistress from the Greek islands.

'And if Harold isn't showing his slides at a Women's Institute meeting next season, I'll eat my hat!' thought Robert, knowing his Thrush Green.

His eyes wandered to the Two Pheasants where the hanging baskets still made a brave splash of colour. Across the expanse of grass, someone was moving among the stones in the grave-yard at St Andrew's, where so many of Robert's old friends, including Mrs Curdle, rested forever.

It looked like the rector, Robert thought, shading his eyes against the sinking sun, and he was about to walk across to greet him, when he heard the front door open behind him, and the sound of voices.

Joan was accompanying Dotty Harmer to the gate, and he turned to greet his old friend, who looked, if anything, even more tattered than usual.

She interrupted her flow of conversation just long enough to say how lovely it was to see him in his own surroundings, and then returned to her discourse.

'Now, I can thoroughly recommend either of the two spaniels. Well, *spaniel-types*, I'd better say. Their tails leave much to be desired, but of course they may fill out as they grow. Both bitches, and a beautiful pale gold.

'I wouldn't suggest the collie. He's going to be enormous, judging by his paws, and I'm trying Percy Hodge for him. I hear he wants another dog, and after all, it was his present collie that was the father. Or *one* of them,' added Dotty, strictly honest.

'That leaves the black and tan terrier-type dog, and the shaggy little bitch. She's going to be *most unusual*, and highly intelligent too. So just think it over, Joan dear. I know whichever you choose will have a marvellous home.'

'Can I bring Paul down to see them when he's home from school? It will really be his puppy. He misses his old dog terribly since she died last winter.'

'Of course, of course.'

She suddenly became conscious of Robert listening with quiet pleasure to the conversation.

'Would you like a puppy, Robert? You'll have all the time in the world now, to train it.'

Robert shook his head.

'I'm too long in the tooth for puppies,' he told her. 'I'll take a share in bringing up Paul's.'

'Very well,' said Dotty, bending to adjust a suspender against her skinny thigh. 'I'll be getting back. Flossie tends to get a little agitated if I'm away for long. Post-natal emotion, of course. Otherwise, she's a wonderful little mother.'

She nodded briskly, and set off across the grass to Lulling Woods, her stockings in imminent danger of collapsing, and one claw-like hand holding on to her disreputable straw hat.

Joan and her father turned back towards their home.

'D'you know,' said Robert, putting an arm round his daughter's shoulders. 'I've thought so often about coming back here. I've thought about the house, and the garden, and the chestnut avenue, and St Andrew's church, and Nathaniel Patten's statue, and all my dear friends here. But the fact is —'

Here he stopped, and drew in his breath.

'The real joy of the place didn't hit me until I saw Mrs Curdle's caravan, and dear old Dotty finding homes, as always, for puppies.

'Now I *know* that I really have returned to Thrush Green.'